Hiya . . .

I am a great believer in dreams. I've had some big dreams myself, so I understand how hard you have to work to turn a dream into reality. What if the hard work is just too much? If the dream turns into an obsession, a nightmare?

Summer Tanberry is popular, pretty, clever and talented. When she is offered the chance of a lifetime, the chance to make her dream come true, she grabs it with both hands, but as the weeks pass and the pressure mounts she finds the dream slipping through her fingers.

How can the 'girl most likely to succeed' find herself so lost, so lonely, so scared? And can 'the most annoying boy in the world' find a way to get through to her?

Summer's Dream is a book for anyone who dreams big or loves dance. It is also a book for anyone who has ever pushed themselves to the limit, dreamed of being the best; and for anyone who has ever looked in the mirror and disliked what they saw there. Summer Tanberry has everything going for her, yet beneath the surface her life is a million miles away from perfect.

Summer's Dream is the third book in the Chocolate Box Girls series. Chill out and lose yourself in the story . . . enjoy!

 xxx

Cathy Cassidy

SUMMER'S DREAM

the chocolate box girls

PUFFIN

PUFFIN BOOKS

Published by the Penguin Group
Penguin Books Ltd, 80 Strand, London WC2R ORL, England
Penguin Group (USA) Inc., 375 Hudson Street, New York, New York 10014, USA
Penguin Group (Canada), 90 Eglinton Avenue East, Suite 700, Toronto, Ontario, Canada M4P 2Y3
(a division of Pearson Penguin Canada Inc.)
Penguin Ireland, 25 St Stephen's Green, Dublin 2, Ireland
(a division of Penguin Books Ltd)
Penguin Group (Australia), 250 Camberwell Road, Camberwell, Victoria 3124, Australia
(a division of Pearson Australia Group Pty Ltd)
Penguin Books India Pvt Ltd, 11 Community Centre, Panchsheel Park, New Delhi – 110 017, India
Penguin Group (NZ), 67 Apollo Drive, Rosedale, Auckland 0632, New Zealand
(a division of Pearson New Zealand Ltd)
Penguin Books (South Africa) (Pty) Ltd, Block D, Rosebank Office Park, 181 Jan Smuts Avenue,
Parktown North, Gauteng 2193, South Africa

Penguin Books Ltd, Registered Offices: 80 Strand, London WC2R ORL, England

puffinbooks.com

First published 2012
Published in this edition 2013
This edition produced for The Book People Ltd,
Hall Wood Avenue, Haydock, St Helens. WA11 9UL
002

Text copyright © Cathy Cassidy, 2012
Illustrations copyright © Puffin Books, 2012
Illustrations by Julie Ingham
All rights reserved

The moral right of the author and illustrator has been asserted

Set in Baskerville by Palimpsest Book Production, Falkirk, Stirlingshire
Printed in Great Britain by Clays Ltd, St Ives plc

British Library Cataloguing in Publication Data
A CIP catalogue record for this book is available from the British Library

ISBN: 978-0-141-34160-6

www.greenpenguin.co.uk

MIX
Paper from
responsible sources
FSC
www.fsc.org   FSC™ C018179

Penguin Books is committed to a sustainable
future for our business, our readers and our planet.
This book is made from Forest Stewardship
Council™ certified paper.

ALWAYS LEARNING   **PEARSON**

Thanks . . .

To Liam, Cal and Caitlin for being . . . well, the best. To Mum, Joan, Andy, Lori and all my brilliant family. Thanks to Helen, Sheena, Fiona, Mary-Jane, Maggi, Lal, Jessie and all of my fab friends for the support, the chocolate, the hugs.

Thanks to my wonderful PA Catriona, to Martyn for the maths and Darley and his team for being both lovely and all-round brilliant. Big hugs to Amanda, my fab and ever-patient editor, and to Sara and Julie for the gorgeous artwork. Thanks also to Adele, Emily, Jayde, Sarah, Julia, Hannah, Samantha, Jane and all the lovely Puffins.

Special thanks to Rachel H, Eva M and many anonymous readers who have helped me to understand Summer's illness a little better. To all my readers, everywhere, thank YOU . . . your enthusiasm and support mean the world to me.

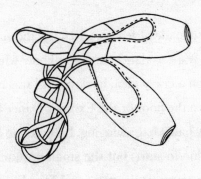

I

Have you ever wanted something so badly that it hurts? I guess we all have, but I am not lusting after a new dress or a kitten or a baby-pink laptop – I wish. No, my dream is bigger than that, and tantalizingly out of reach.

It's not even an unusual dream – loads of little girls probably share the exact same one. Anybody who ever went to dance class or dressed up in fairy wings and skipped about the living room probably hopes that one day they'll be up on stage with the audience throwing red roses at their feet. For me, the dream stuck; it hasn't been replaced by a passion for ponies, for pop stars, for boys. Even though I have a boyfriend these days, the dream hasn't wavered one bit.

I want to be a dancer, a ballerina, to dance the part of Giselle or Coppélia or Juliet, to dress up as the swan princess in a white tutu made of feathers, to make the audience gasp and cheer. I want to dance, and you know what? It didn't seem like such a crazy idea, back when I was nine or ten.

I push open the door of the Exmoor Dance Studios and go inside, my ballet bag swinging. It's early, an hour before my class is due to start, but the small upstairs studio the seniors use is empty at this time and Miss Elise has always told me I am welcome to use it whenever I like.

I do like, quite a lot, these days.

The foyer is busy with little girls in pink leotards, laughing, talking, buying juice and biscuits as a treat between school and dance class, or queuing with their mums to book up for the summer holiday sessions. I used to be just like them, once.

I was good. I got distinctions in every exam I took, danced centre stage at every dance school show, got used to Miss Elise telling the class, 'No, no, girls, pay attention – look at Summer! Why can't you all dance like that?'

My twin sister, Skye, used to roll her eyes and stick her tongue out at me, and the minute Miss Elise's back was turned the whole class would fall about giggling.

Don't get me wrong, though – dance was one thing I

always took seriously, even if Skye didn't. I loved it. I signed up for every class the dance school offered: tap, modern, jazz, street . . . but ballet was my first love, always. At home I devoured ballet books about girls who overcame the odds to make their dreams come true. My poster girl was Angelina Ballerina, and I watched my DVD of *Billy Elliot* so many times I wore it out. When I wasn't reading about dance or watching DVDs or dreaming about it, I was practising because even then I knew that being good was not enough; I had to be the best.

Dad called me his little ballerina, and I loved that. When you have lots of sisters – clever, talented sisters – you have to try a little harder than most to be noticed. I guess I'm a bit of a perfectionist.

Miss Elise told Mum she thought I was good enough to audition for the Royal Ballet School, that she would set up the auditions for when I was eleven. I was so excited I thought I might explode. I could see a whole future stretching before me, a future of pointe shoes and leotards and aching muscles, a future that could end with me in a feathered tutu on the stage at the Royal Opera House.

It was so close I could almost reach out and touch it.

And then everything fell apart. Dad left us and moved up to London and it was like our whole family crumbled. For months Mum looked hopeless and crushed, and there were rows about visits with Dad, rows about maintenance payments, rows about everything. My big sister Honey raged and blamed Mum for what had happened.

'I bet Dad thinks she doesn't love him any more,' Honey told us. 'They've been arguing loads. Dad can't help it if he has to be away a lot, he's a businessman! Mum nags too much – she's driven him away!'

I wasn't sure about that, though. It seemed to me that Dad had been spending less time with us and more time in London for a while now. Mum didn't so much nag as mention quietly that it'd be great if he could be around for Coco's birthday or Easter Sunday or even Father's Day, and that would trigger a big scrap, with Dad shouting and slamming doors and Mum in tears.

When I asked Dad why he was leaving, he said that he still loved us, very much, but things hadn't been perfect for a while now. Back then it didn't seem like a good enough reason to me. When things aren't perfect, you need to work at them until they are, right? Dad obviously had different ideas.

❀❀❀❀❀❀❀❀❀❀❀❀❀❀❀❀❀❀❀

A few days after the split, Skye, my twin, announced that she didn't want to go to ballet class any more, that she'd only really gone along with it because I wanted to go. That kind of pulled the rug out from under my feet. I always thought that Skye and I knew everything there was to know about each other . . . and it turned out I was wrong. Skye had a whole bunch of ideas that I didn't know about.

'Summer, I don't want to tag along in your shadow any more,' she said, and if she'd slapped my face, I couldn't have been more hurt. It felt like she was cutting loose, leaving me stranded, at exactly the moment I needed her most.

If you'd taken my life and shaken it up and thrown the smashed-up pieces down in a temper, you couldn't have made more of a mess. So . . . yeah, that whole ballet school idea. It was never going to take off after Dad left, I could see that.

I passed the regional auditions OK, but by the time the date rolled around for the London one my head was a muddle of worries and fears. Could I really leave Mum, so soon after the break-up? Could I leave my sisters? I was torn.

5

❀❀❀❀❀❀❀❀❀❀❀❀❀❀❀❀❀❀❀❀❀

Dad had agreed to take me to the audition, being based in London himself, but he was late collecting me and by the time we finally arrived I was sick with nerves. I danced badly, and when the panel asked me why I thought I should be given a place at the Royal Ballet School, I couldn't think of a single reason.

'Never mind,' Dad said, exasperated, driving me home. 'It's no big deal. Ballet is just a hobby really, isn't it?'

That just about killed me. Ballet was a big deal to me – it was everything. I stopped being Dad's 'little ballerina' that day. I'd lost his respect – I was just one daughter of several after that, the one whose hobby was dance.

Needless to say, I wasn't offered a place.

'Don't blame yourself,' Mum told me. 'You've been under a lot of pressure, and I should never have trusted your dad to get you there on time. There'll be other chances.'

I smiled, but we both knew that I'd messed up a once-in-a-lifetime opportunity.

You'd never have made it anyway, a sad, sour voice whispered inside my head. *You were kidding yourself.*

I brushed the voice aside, although I couldn't quite forget it. Sure enough, that voice has been around ever since, chipping into my thoughts with a bitter put-down whenever I least expect it.

That was over two years ago. Now, I am thirteen and I still love to dance. I still get distinctions in my exams and I still get good roles in the shows. Things at home are better. Dad lives in Australia now, but it's not like we saw much of him anyway, even before the move. Mum has a new boyfriend, Paddy, who is kind and funny and easy to like. They are getting married in just a few days' time. Paddy has a daughter, Cherry, so I have a new stepsister too, and I like her lots.

My big sister Honey can still be a nightmare, especially since Paddy and Cherry moved in, but I have Skye and Coco, a boyfriend, and good friends I can rely on. I do well at school. I should be happy, I know . . . but I'm not. Even though I messed up my chance of dancing professionally, I still have that dream.

In the deserted changing room beside the senior studio, I peel off my school uniform and fold it neatly, wriggling into tights and leotard. It's like peeling away the layers of the real world. In my dance clothes I feel light, clean, free.

I loosen my hair from its long plaits, brush away the day's

hassles and braid it again tightly, pinning it up around my head. I have done this so many times I don't even need a mirror any more. I sit down on the wooden bench and pull the pointe shoes out of my bag. I slip my feet into the pink satin shoes and tie the ribbons firmly, tucking the ends out of sight the way Miss Elise has taught me. I stand and walk across the changing room, into the empty studio, the mirrors glinting. Beside the door, I dip the toes of my shoes into the chalky dust of the rosin box, so that I do not slip or slide on the hardwood floor. I reach down and flick on the CD player and the music unfurls around me, seeping under my skin.

When I dance, my troubles fall away. It doesn't matter that Dad left and that my family are still putting the pieces back together again. It doesn't even matter that I never got to go to the Royal Ballet School.

I take a deep breath and run forward, rising up en pointe, curving my arms upwards, swooping, twirling, losing myself in the music. When I dance, the world disappears, and everything is finally perfect.

2

'Summer!' my twin yells through from the bedroom. 'Can you help me with my hair?'

I glance into the bathroom mirror and smooth down my white lace dress, frowning. The dress is a copy of a vintage petticoat, and all five of us sisters are wearing the same style, each with a satin sash in different ice-cream colours. Skye loves vintage, but this dress is not one I'd ever have chosen. It looks wrong on me somehow, too lumpy, too gathered, making me look bigger than I really am. I'm starting to hate all my clothes lately . . . or is it my shape I don't like?

'Summer?' Skye calls again.

'OK, I'm coming!'

Skye has woven a circlet of soft-pink mallow flowers and trailing baby-blue ribbon for her hair and she needs my help to fix it in place. My hair is simpler, left loose and wavy with just a pink silk flower pinned on one side. The flower was a gift from my boyfriend Aaron last Christmas. That was before he was actually my boyfriend, of course. I found the prettily wrapped present labelled 'from a secret admirer' in my locker at school – it's probably the most romantic thing Aaron's ever done. He is not a slushy kind of boy and he has never mentioned the flower at all, but still, I love it.

'We look OK, don't we?' Skye says. 'For bridesmaids!'

'Not a nylon ruffle in sight,' I agree. 'But . . . you don't think the dress makes me look . . . well, too curvy, do you?'

'Too curvy?' Skye echoes. 'No way, Summer! You're really slim, you know you are! Besides, we're meant to have curves. That's part of growing up.'

'I'm not sure I like it,' I sigh. 'When I look in the mirror these days, it doesn't even look like me.'

'Well, it is,' Skye says. 'And it's me too – we're identical twins, remember? I know what you mean, though. It takes a bit of getting used to!'

She sticks her tongue out at her reflection, and the two of us burst out laughing together.

'I can't wait to see Mum's dress!' I say. 'She's been so

strict about keeping it secret. She actually made Paddy sleep in the gypsy caravan last night!'

'It's bad luck for a bridegroom to see the wedding dress before the big moment,' Skye says. 'And Mum and Paddy don't need any more of that!'

Skye is right. Paddy's first wife died when his daughter Cherry was just a toddler, and Mum has had it rough too, what with Dad leaving. We're all hoping this wedding will be the start of happier times.

The door swings open and Coco comes in, dragging Humbug, her pet lamb, on a leash. 'Should I make a flower garland for Humbug's collar?' she asks. 'So that she looks pretty for the wedding? Or would she just eat it, d'you think?'

'Eat it,' Skye and I say together.

'Definitely,' I add, peering out of the window. 'That lamb is a walking, bleating waste-disposal unit. Oh . . . look! JJ's here with the horse . . . It's the dappled grey one!'

JJ's dad owns the farm next door, and Mum and Paddy are borrowing one of their horses to pull the gypsy caravan.

'He's early!' Coco squeaks. 'I'm going down!' She clatters down the stairs, Humbug at her heels.

I press my face against the glass, looking down at the

garden. Some blokes I've never seen before are draping fairy lights and bunting through the trees. A car pulls up and Paddy wanders across the grass towards it, his hair sticking up in unruly clumps, carrying a pair of new Converse trainers and his wedding suit over one arm.

'The best man's come to collect Paddy,' I say. 'That's it then . . . not long now!'

Since early this morning Tanglewood has been in total chaos. The house is stuffed with Mum's friends and relatives instead of our usual B&B guests, and when Skye and I went downstairs earlier, we found a crowd of women eating bacon and eggs at the kitchen table in their pyjamas, friends of Mum's from her art college days. There were two great-aunts from Yorkshire trying on scary wedding hats in the living room, and a tribe of children smeared with chocolate spread, the offspring of distant cousins. In the middle of it all, Grandma Kate was calmly making cheese scones; her husband Jules (who's not really my grandad, but sort of is now) was buttering bread.

'Maybe we should go down and help with the food,' Skye says now, reading my mind.

We get ambushed halfway down the stairs by Honey, her

white dress adjusted so it's pretty much a mini, jaw-length blonde hair ruffled as if she has just got out of bed. She blinks at me over armfuls of garden flowers, blue eyes fringed with sooty mascara, model-girl cool.

'Grandma Kate has put me in charge of the flowers,' she says. 'I know this is a shoestring wedding, but why scrimp on style? I've ransacked the garden. Can you two help make posies?'

Honey dumps the flowers in the bathroom sink before heading out to forage for more. Skye and I start making posies and Cherry joins in too, snipping bright carnations for buttonholes and twisting wire and silver foil around the stems. Cherry has given the petticoat dress her own cool twist, accessorizing with a Japanese parasol and chopsticks in her hair. Her mum was Japanese, so the look fits.

'Dad's gone into Kitnor with Uncle Shaun to get ready,' she says. 'He was SO nervous . . .'

'He should be,' Honey says, coming up behind us with a final haul of flowers. 'If he ever hurts Mum, I'll happily strangle him myself. No offence, obviously.'

'Obviously,' Cherry says, through gritted teeth.

The wedding was always going to be difficult for Honey.

She doesn't like Paddy and she can't stand Cherry either, especially since our new stepsister started dating Honey's ex. Avoiding bloodshed, catfights and major rows was always going to be a challenge today, but I suppose at least it's limited to snide comments rather than door-slamming and screaming.

Across the landing, one of the art school friends appears carrying hairspray and curling tongs into Mum's room. I catch the door before it swings shut, and we peep through to catch a glimpse of Mum having her make-up done. She looks so lovely that the breath catches in my throat.

'Oh, girls!' she says, face lighting up at the sight of us. 'You look fabulous!'

'Not as fabulous as you, Mum!' I tell her.

Then the art school friends usher us away, closing the door firmly. My sisters are taking this houseful of strangers in their stride, but I can't help feeling a little shut out, a little stressed by the chaos. I like things to be neat, orderly, under control . . . and they hardly ever are, not in this house. Today especially.

'Scram,' Honey says. 'I want to get Mum's bouquet done.'

14

Skye, Cherry and I go downstairs to clear up the kitchen, chasing Grandma Kate and Jules off to get changed. Outside, trestle tables, folding chairs and picnic blankets have appeared, scattered across the grass, and random relatives wander through the kitchen carrying tablecloths, plates and cutlery.

'I wish it wasn't such a muddle,' I frown, stacking the dishwasher as Cherry hands out buttonholes and posies. 'We're supposed to be leaving in a few minutes . . .'

'We will,' Skye laughs. 'Relax!'

People begin to gather on the lawn, the chocolate-spread children, cleaned up to an angelic shine, the Yorkshire aunts like garish, well-upholstered sofas, scary hats balanced on tightly curled grey hair. JJ drives the gypsy caravan right up to the house and jumps down to hold the dappled grey horse. Someone has twined a string of tiny bells through her harness – I suspect it was probably Coco.

Grandma Kate and Jules appear, smiling and proud, and Grandma Kate takes the reins and climbs up on to the caravan step. Our real grandad died before Skye and I were born, so Grandma Kate is giving Mum away. She knows how to drive the wagon because she used to do it, years ago, when she lived here at Tanglewood.

15

✿✿✿✿✿✿✿✿✿✿✿✿✿✿✿✿✿✿✿✿

'Here they come!' someone yells, and then the art school friends spill out of the house, a riot of bright hair and red lippy, and finally Mum is in the doorway.

Her hair is pinned up in a loose, messy bun with corkscrew curls falling down around her face, tiny blue flowers threaded into the tawny-blonde waves. Her dress is a gorgeous, vintage-inspired sheath of soft white velvet; her tanned legs are bare and on her feet she wears jewelled flip-flops that cost £2.99 in a cut-price shoe shop in Minehead. She is holding a spray of starry white jasmine and roses tied with ribbon and her face is lit up with happiness and hope.

My heart swells with pride. I am happy for Mum, I really am, but sad too, for the family we used to be. Everything is changing, and I am not sure I like change.

Jules helps Mum up on to the wagon seat, Grandma Kate snaps the reins and the dappled grey horse moves forward, jingling, down towards the church.

3

We walk down to the village behind the gypsy wagon, brides-maids first and everyone else following. It is slightly weird to be at your own mum's wedding, but there's lots of laughter and chat, as if we are setting off for some kind of crazy family picnic. When we pass the inn at the edge of the village, Paddy's musician friends from Scotland latch on, playing guitar and fiddle and flute, so we arrive at the church in style.

The aunts and cousins and art school friends file into the church to the sound of leaping Scottish fiddle music while the rest of us gather on the church steps. Mum smoothes down her white velvet dress and tucks a stray ringlet behind her ear.

The church is full to the brim and Paddy and his brother

are standing down at the altar with the vicar. Then the church organ strikes up 'Here Comes the Bride', and Grandma Kate takes Mum's arm and the two of them walk inside and move slowly down the aisle with us following along behind.

All eyes are on us, and even though I have had my moments in the spotlight, this is a whole lot more nerve-wracking. On stage I am a performer, hiding behind a role, lost in the dance. Here I'm just me, with nothing to hide behind, awkward in a petticoat dress I'd never have picked out for myself. Two spots of colour burn in my cheeks, but I link Skye's arm and we fall into step together.

We squash into the front seats, Coco struggling to keep Humbug the lamb on a short leash, and the ceremony starts. It all goes smoothly, and then we get to the point where the vicar asks whether anyone has any reason why Mum and Paddy should not be legally wed, and I look around anxiously in case Dad should stride suddenly into the church to object. Of course he doesn't because a) he is in Australia and b) he doesn't care whether Mum gets married or not. All that actually happens is that Honey whispers, 'Because Paddy is a jerk,' under her breath, but luckily nobody hears except me.

❀❀❀❀❀❀❀❀❀❀❀❀❀❀❀❀❀❀❀❀❀❀❀

When I was younger, I used to think Dad would change his mind about the divorce, see that he couldn't live without us and swoop back in with armfuls of flowers and apologies to put things back together again. He never did, of course, and I started to see that happy endings aren't always the way you think they'll be.

The vicar announces that Paddy and Mum are man and wife, and then they're kissing and Coco says 'Eeeewww!' and everyone laughs. I swallow back a knot of emotion that is part sadness for what might have been and part happiness for Mum, and I hope that nobody else can see the conflict in my eyes. My dad won't win any awards for 'best dad in the universe', that's for sure, but I can't help wishing, sometimes, that I could turn the clock back. I'd try a little harder to make him love me, to make him proud, and maybe then he'd have stayed.

Or maybe not.

We crowd out on to the church steps in a blizzard of confetti, and the next half-hour is a blur of smiles and photos . . . standing on the steps, standing under the trees, posing with the gypsy caravan while JJ holds the horse and shoots flirty glances at Honey.

At last, Mum and Paddy climb up into the wagon seat. Paddy twitches the reins and the dappled grey horse breaks into a trot as Mum throws her flowers into the crowd. They say that whoever catches the bride's bouquet will be next down the aisle, and one of the Yorkshire aunts makes a lunge for it and hangs on tight. She is in her seventies and has never married, so this causes a stir, especially when she giggles and says she has her eye on the vicar.

Back at Tanglewood, the party unfolds. The garden is filled with people hugging Mum and Paddy, handing over presents, helping themselves to the buffet. People who weren't at the church service begin to arrive too, friends and neighbours from the village, Tia and Millie from school, Mrs Lee from the post office, and even Mr and Mrs Anderson from the health-food store, with their hippy-dippy clothes and their cute little girls and their deeply annoying son Alfie who seems to be making it his life's work to bug me.

'Cool wedding,' Alfie remarks. 'I like your dress, Summer . . .'

I roll my eyes. 'Like your dress' is probably Alfie Anderson code for 'you look like you're wearing a net curtain'. That boy has been winding me up since the day we first met, back in Reception class, when he came up to me in the lunch queue and asked if I'd be his girlfriend, then blew a raspberry right in my ear and made me drop my rice pudding and jam.

I have never really forgiven him for that.

'Get lost, Alfie,' I say.

And then I am rescued because someone slides their hands over my eyes and whispers 'Guess who?' into my hair.

Sometimes I think I must be the luckiest girl in the world, because Aaron Jones is the cutest boy at Exmoor Park Middle School and every girl in my year has been crushing on him since forever. And he chose me.

'Aaron,' I grin. 'Who else?'

He takes my hands and spins me round, laughing. 'How did it go?' he asks. 'Cool, I bet. Nice dress . . . clingy . . . it really shows off your figure!'

I blush furiously and try to fold my arms over my chest, but Aaron is laughing. 'That's a good thing, Summer! This is an amazing party – have you eaten yet?'

'I wasn't hungry . . . my tummy's all butterflies . . .'

He hands me a plate and takes one himself, piling it up with sausage rolls and quiche and a mountain of potato salad. 'Nerves,' he says wisely. 'It's a big day for your family, Summer. I get like that before a footy match sometimes. Then afterwards, I could eat for Britain. This pizza looks amazing . . .'

I reach out to take a slice, then remember Aaron's remark about my figure and take a forkful of salad leaves instead.

The music dies and the best man takes hold of the mike. He talks about how Mum and Paddy were friends way back at art college, then found each other again so many years later and fell in love. He says that Mum must be crazy to put up with Paddy. 'Either that or she's fallen in love with his chocolate-making skills,' he says, and tells everyone how Paddy used to send Mum home-made truffles to woo her.

'The best one was the truffle Paddy made for me last August, just after he and Cherry moved down here,' Mum chips in. 'It was the day we got our bank loan for the chocolate business. Paddy made my favourite coffee truffle, but there was an extra ingredient, one I really hadn't expected . . .'

She holds out her left hand so that the diamond engagement ring glints in the sunlight, a plain gold band now next to it, and everyone cheers and whistles. I remember that day – I thought that hiding the ring inside a chocolate was the most romantic thing I'd ever seen.

Aaron slides an arm round my waist, and I smile and wriggle free again because I am still a little shy about the dress, and besides, I am actually not too good at the touchy-feely boyfriend/girlfriend stuff. Not yet, and definitely not while people are watching.

Mum and Paddy cut the towering chocolate wedding cake and Jules and the Yorkshire aunts move through the crowd, topping up champagne glasses and handing out lemonade punch for the kids. Grandma Kate raises her glass to make a toast, then Paddy's musician friends strike up a tune and Paddy takes Mum's hand and leads her out across the grass. They begin to dance, slowly, gazing into each other's eyes and smiling so softly I swear it would melt a heart of stone.

It melts mine, and I push all thoughts of Dad away because they can only end in tears. Today is a day for Mum and Paddy, for new starts and celebrations.

Honey's heart must be harder than mine, though, because I see her slip away through the cherry trees with JJ, making pukey faces at it all.

4

The party goes on till past midnight, beneath the stars and the fairy lights strung through the trees. I dance with Skye and Cherry and Coco. I dance with Tia and Millie and the little cousins who are hyper and giggling from too many cupcakes and too much lemonade punch. I waltz with the Yorkshire aunts and boogie with Mum's art school friends and jig with Paddy's musician mates. Last of all, I slow-dance with Aaron and he holds me close, closer than I really want to be held, and tells me I am the prettiest girl he has ever dated.

It makes my heart race, although whether from happiness or panic I can't quite tell. Aaron has had a few girlfriends in the past, and there's even a rumour that a girl from the high school called Marisa McKenna is crushing on him. Marisa wears her skirts so short it sometimes looks like she's forgotten to put one on at all, but when I asked Aaron about her, he laughed and told me that the only girl he wanted was me.

'Are you and Aaron in love?' my twin asks later, as we snuggle down in our beds, music and laughter still drifting up from the garden below. 'What's it like, Summer? Honestly?'

I frown in the darkness. I like Aaron a lot, of course – who wouldn't? I'm just not sure I love him. Not true love, like Mum and Paddy have.

'I don't know,' I tell Skye. 'It's early days.'

'It's been four months,' Skye points out. 'You must have some idea. Does he make your heart beat faster? Does he make you melt inside? Do you lie awake, tossing and turning, thinking about him?'

'You make it sound like some kind of sickness,' I say. 'It's complicated . . . Aaron's been out with lots of girls. I worry that he'll move on, find someone he likes better . . .'

Someone who's better at the kissing and cuddling stuff, who doesn't flinch away when he pulls them close. In real life, kissing isn't as dreamy as the magazines make out. You worry about whether your noses will bump, whether your teeth will clash, whether the pasta sauce you had for tea is making your breath smell of onions. You feel awkward, anxious, slightly bored . . . at least I do.

'He won't,' Skye says. 'He's mad about you, anyone can see that!'

I sigh in the darkness. 'Maybe.'

'D'you think a boy will feel that way about me some day?' Skye asks softly.

'Of course!'

It's only later, when Skye's breathing has slowed into sleep, that I think to wonder if she has a particular boy in mind.

The next day, the house is filled with sleepy relatives and art school friends with hangovers and sticky-up hair, clearing up slowly, gathering bottles and cans for the recycling centre, stacking and unstacking the dishwasher a dozen times. We find a stiletto shoe floating in the fish pond, a bottle of whisky hidden in the flower bed and the best man asleep in the gypsy caravan wearing nothing but a pair of polka-dot boxer shorts, mirrored sunglasses and a trilby hat.

❀❀❀❀❀❀❀❀❀❀❀❀❀❀❀❀❀❀❀❀❀

'Great party,' Paddy grins. 'What I can remember of it anyhow!'

'Aren't you two supposed to be on honeymoon?' I tease, mopping the kitchen floor. 'It's traditional, you know!'

'And miss our own wedding party?' Paddy retorts. 'No chance!'

'No money, more like,' Mum says. 'Besides, we've you girls to look after, and the B&B and the chocolate business to run!'

'I may have something up my sleeve for once the school holidays start,' Paddy hints, and Mum says she won't hold her breath because most likely it will be a day trip to Minehead, and everyone laughs.

Morning slides into afternoon, and people begin to pack up and head for home. By evening, all our guests are gone except for Grandma Kate and Jules, and it feels like the house is ours again.

I take time out to run through some ballet exercises in my bedroom because I missed yesterday's lesson and I get restless and edgy if I don't practise. I love the way my body feels as it spins and stretches, strong and light and powerful. I love the way the music fills my head, my heart. Dancing is like a cleaner, simpler version of life. I know the rules. I don't have to worry about unflattering dresses or boyfriends who want to dance too close.

I dance until my muscles ache, until the smell of roast chicken wafts up the stairs and Mum calls me down to eat. Everyone is sitting round the kitchen table, even Honey, who vanished from the party early on yesterday and escaped the clean-up duties today by hiding out in her room.

'Well,' Paddy says as he carves the chicken. 'What a weekend! You've made me the happiest man alive, Charlotte, and girls . . . Kate, Jules . . . well, thanks, all of you, for making Cherry and me so welcome here. I guess we're a proper family now.'

Honey snorts her disgust, but I nudge her underneath the table and she bites her tongue.

'So . . . Minehead for the honeymoon, is it?' Grandma Kate grins.

'I don't care,' Mum shrugs. 'I'd be happy anywhere with Paddy.'

'Good,' Paddy says. 'Because Kate and Jules have a surprise for you . . .'

'A surprise?' Mum echoes. 'What kind of a surprise?'

❀❀❀❀❀❀❀❀❀❀❀❀❀❀❀❀❀❀❀

'We want to send you on honeymoon,' Grandma Kate says. 'You deserve it after all the hard work you've put in on the B&B and the chocolate business. We want to give you a holiday to remember, something special . . . It's our wedding present to you both. We talked to Paddy and between us we've arranged it all . . .'

'Arranged what?' Mum says.

Grandma Kate pushes a thick white envelope across the table, and Mum opens it, frowning. There are two tickets, a sheaf of printed itineraries and a glossy holiday brochure inside.

For Peru.

Mum's eyes brim with tears. 'I – I don't understand! Three weeks in Peru? It's wonderful, but we can't accept. Mum, Jules, you can't possibly . . . and besides, we can't leave the girls . . . or the business . . . and don't forget the film crew are using Tanglewood as a base this summer! I don't see how we can do it!'

'It's all planned,' Jules says. 'Paddy has hired an assistant for the chocolate business and Kate will come over and look after the girls while you're away . . .'

'The film crew will be here, yes,' Grandma Kate adds.

❀❀❀❀❀❀❀❀❀❀❀❀❀❀❀❀❀❀❀

'But they'll be pretty self-sufficient, and the B&B would have to be closed anyway while they're at Tanglewood. Come on, Charlotte . . . you've always dreamt of going to Peru!'

'Well, yes,' Mum whispers. 'I'd love to go, of course. I've always wanted to, and Paddy and I have talked about it too, because of the chocolate business . . .'

'We pay more to get ethically sourced cocoa beans,' Paddy says. 'But this could be our chance to take it further . . . support a small family plantation, fairly traded, organic. All that, and the trip of a lifetime too!'

'Well, yes,' Mum says. 'But . . .'

Paddy puts an arm round her shoulders. 'No buts,' he says. 'It's all sorted. We fly out the first weekend of the school holidays. Kate will be here, and the kids are old enough to be responsible, behave well and help out if they're needed. Right, girls?'

'Right!' Skye agrees. 'We'll be fine, won't we?'

'Fine,' I chime in, but actually I am not sure just how fine I will be if Mum and Paddy vanish off to Peru for three weeks. It sounds like a brilliant honeymoon and it's really generous of Grandma Kate and Jules, but I can't help wishing they'd asked us how we'd feel about it first.

30

❁❁❁❁❁❁❁❁❁❁❁❁❁❁❁❁❁❁❁

I push my dinner away, half eaten. I already have a dad who lives on the other side of the world – I am not sure I want Mum disappearing too, even if it is only for three weeks. I can't say that, though – it would sound horribly mean and selfish.

Besides, it looks like I'm the only one with doubts.

'Wow,' Honey is saying. 'Mum, look, I haven't made things easy for you lately . . . I probably haven't been as welcoming to Paddy or Cherry as I could have been . . .'

Cherry's eyes widen. This is the understatement of the year, or possibly the century.

'I suppose I'm trying to say sorry,' Honey says brightly. 'I've been a pain, but that's all over now. We'll be fine while you go on honeymoon – you have to go, Mum, you know that, yeah? When will you ever get another chance like this?'

'Exactly,' Grandma Kate says.

I exchange glances with Skye. We've waited forever for Honey to sweeten up a little . . . but now that it's actually happening I can't help wondering if it's for real. My big sister knows how to turn on the charm when she wants to, and Mum and Grandma Kate fall for it every time. Me, I'm not so sure.

31

The conversation turns to passports and packing and cocoa plantations in Peru. I wish I could be excited too, but instead, I feel anxious, uncertain, adrift.

'*Yesss*,' my big sister whispers under her breath. 'Three weeks of freedom. This is going to be the best summer holiday ever . . .'

I have a bad feeling about this . . . a very bad feeling indeed.

The Fire Bird

5

Learning to dance en pointe is tough. It takes years and years to build up the strength, years of discipline and exercise. Even now, I try to do 100 relevés every day to keep my feet and ankles strong. Miss Elise calls them 'killers' and I know exactly why.

It takes sheer stamina to make pointe work look so light, so easy, so free. The first few times I tried it, my toes blistered and bled and my toenails were bruised black and blue. I didn't complain, though – ballerinas don't.

I am running through my barre work in the empty senior studio when the door creaks open and my friend Jodie walks in. Jodie lives out on the other side of Minehead and goes to school in a different town. When it comes to dance, Jodie is good. She is the only person I know who takes dance as seriously as I do.

Once upon a time we both shared the same dreams of going to the Royal Ballet School, but of course those dreams didn't come to anything. For me it was because I arrived late and flustered and danced badly, but for Jodie it was crueller still. The panel said that Jodie had natural grace and talent, but that her body shape wasn't quite right for a professional dancer.

'What does that even mean?' Jodie had asked me later, her face stained with tears. 'Do I have an extra head or something?'

Jodie looked fine to me. She wasn't too tall or too small, too fat or too thin. Her posture was good, her muscles strong. I wiped her tears and told her to forget it, but it turned out those experts knew more than we did. As Jodie slid into puberty, her body changed – her boobs are big, her tummy rounded, her legs strong and solid. In everyday clothes, she looks stunning, curvy and soft and sweet. The panel were right, though. She doesn't look like a dancer.

We stopped talking about our ballerina dreams, but mine didn't go away and I'm pretty sure Jodie's didn't either. The two of us aren't even in the same class these days – Miss Elise moved me up a grade in January to dance with the seniors, so I'm surprised and pleased to see Jodie now.

'Hey,' I grin. 'What's up? I didn't expect to see you here!'

Jodie smiles. 'Miss Elise has asked me to dance with the senior class today. I think she invited some Grade Six students along too . . . someone told me she had a friend coming in to observe, and she wants to impress her.'

'Oh! I wish she'd told us!' I frown. 'I could have prepared a little more. I hate it when she springs things on us like that. Who is this friend? D'you think it might be someone to take over Miss Laura's class when she goes off on maternity leave?'

'No idea,' Jodie shrugs. 'I'm so nervous, though, dancing with the seniors – I thought I'd do some warm-ups first. If I can impress Miss Elise, she might move me up, like she did with you. She says I'm just about ready to dance en pointe!'

'Brilliant!' I say. 'I hope she does – that would be so cool!'

'Does it hurt?' she asks. 'Pointe work?'

'A little bit, at first,' I shrug. 'It's worth it, though. And after a while, it doesn't hurt any more.'

❀❀❀❀❀❀❀❀❀❀❀❀❀❀❀❀❀❀

Jodie nods. She positions herself at the bar and runs through her exercises, and by the time the others begin coming through for class the two of us have been working together for a good half an hour, companionable, focused, content.

As Jodie predicts, a couple of Grade Six students and even one from Grade Five turn up, and Miss Elise's visitor turns out to be a slim, graceful older woman, greying hair scraped back into a ballerina bun.

'This is my very dear friend Sylvie,' Miss Elise tells us. 'She's a dance teacher too, and I wanted her to observe one of our classes. I know you will dance your very best for her!'

I stand a little straighter, tilting my chin, and when the music begins, I let it seep into me. My limbs are light as silk and as strong as steel, my body taut as wire yet supple as a tree branch bending in the breeze. In the background, I can hear Miss Elise calling out her usual commentary: 'Lucy, watch those toes! Jasmine, concentrate – you're losing the rhythm! Sushila, stretch that leg . . . push yourself! Work, Amanda! You're dreaming! Jodie, excellent, keep going!'

She doesn't say anything about me, and after a while, I lose myself in the music, forget about Miss Elise and her friend, forget about Jodie, forget everything but the dance.

Afterwards, the changing room is thick with bodyspray and gossip.

'I wonder why Miss Elise brought her friend to see us dance,' Jodie wonders. 'I bet she's going to cover for Miss Laura while she's away. She looked strict, but I think she knows what she's doing. She watched you for a long time, Summer, and she was watching me too. We both danced well today!'

'D'you think she's been a professional dancer?' I ask. 'She had that look about her. The way she carried herself. Perhaps she'll take the senior class for some lessons – it might be good to have a different teacher! A challenge!'

Miss Elise appears in the doorway. She asks Jodie, Sushila and me to come along to the office as soon as we are ready, and the three of us exchange anxious glances as we tidy our hair and pick up our ballet bags.

Sushila is one of the senior girls. 'Are we in trouble?' she wonders. 'Miss Elise kept telling me to push myself, work harder!'

'But she said Jodie was dancing well,' I point out. 'And she didn't mention me at all. We can't all be in trouble, surely?'

All the same, there is a knot of anxiety in my belly as we knock at the office door.

'Girls! Come in,' Miss Elise says.

It's more of a sitting room than an office. The last time I came in here was when Mum was late paying my fees the year Dad left and we sat together on the sofa and listened as Miss Elise told us she was not prepared to lose a dancer like me, fees or no fees, and that Mum could take as long as she needed to pay. Mum sold her bicycle and paid the fees the next day, but I'll never forget Miss Elise's kindness. She knew how awful it would be for me if I couldn't dance.

Miss Elise and her friend are sitting in armchairs, sipping tea from pretty china cups. Miss Elise waves us over to the sofa and we perch awkwardly as she pours three glasses of weak squash and arranges Rich Tea biscuits on a plate.

'Sushila, Jodie, Summer . . . I'd like you to meet Sylvie Rochelle,' she says. 'She was most impressed with you all in class today. Well done!'

'Thank you, Miss Elise!' Jodie says, beaming. 'Thank you, Miss . . . um . . . Rochelle.'

'Thank you,' Sushila echoes.

But my manners have deserted me because the name

Sylvie Rochelle is one I have heard before, and when I look at the elegant woman smiling at me over her teacup, I know exactly why. It was the grey hair that confused me. In the poster on my bedroom wall, Sylvie Rochelle has black hair that falls in soft wings about her ears, a cap of dark red flowers and a tutu of crimson silk and net.

'Sylvie Rochelle,' I whisper. 'You danced with the Royal Ballet in the 1970s! I have a picture of you in *The Firebird*!'

'Ah, yes . . .' Sylvie smiles, and her voice is slow and heavily accented, just like Grandad Jules. 'A long time ago, of course. I danced with some of the smaller French companies after that, but for the last fifteen years I've been teaching, first in France and then at the Royal Ballet School.'

'Wow,' I say. 'I mean . . . wow!'

'For a year or so now, Sylvie has been working on a project of her own,' Miss Elise tells us. 'An independent dance school in Devon, for boarders, like the Royal Ballet School but with a more European flavour. Sylvie has been renovating an old girls' school, installing a state-of-the-art theatre and studios, recruiting teachers from around the world ready for the first intake this September . . .'

Jodie bites into a Rich Tea biscuit, her eyes wide, and

❀❀❀❀❀❀❀❀❀❀❀❀❀❀❀❀❀❀❀❀❀❀

Sushila chokes on her orange squash. Me, I hardly dare breathe.

'Elise 'as been a very good friend to me,' Sylvie Rochelle shrugs. 'She 'as been saying for some time that there is a need for a residential ballet school with a more . . . well, cosmopolitan feel to it? When she told me she 'ad some pupils she wanted me to take a look at, I was only too 'appy to comply. We are auditioning for the last few scholarship places at Rochelle Academy this August. I would like it very much if you three girls would try out.'

'No way!' Sushila says.

'Me?' Jodie stutters. 'Really? Me?'

I can't say a thing.

'It's just an audition,' Miss Elise points out. 'There will be other girls going for those places too – the competition will be stiff. If you're offered a scholarship place, be very clear – it will be on your own merits. Sylvie is looking for dedication and potential, for students who will work hard, put dance above everything else. If you're not willing to do that, these auditions are not for you.'

'We are,' I say instantly. 'We will, I promise you.'

'You 'ave eight weeks to prepare for the auditions,' Sylvie

Rochelle says, putting down her teacup neatly. 'Don't waste that time. Each of you 'as talent, but I need to see more. I need to see potential, passion, hunger for success. You must convince me that one of those places should be yours.'

My heart is racing, my eyes shining. When I messed up that audition for the Royal Ballet School, I thought it was the end of my dream, but the dream refused to give up on me. Sometimes I think it is all that has been keeping me afloat these last couple of years. I never stopped working, never stopped hoping, and I promised myself that if I was ever given a second chance, I would grab it with both hands and hold on tight.

You'd have to be crazy to let a dream slip through your fingers all over again, right?

6

When I get back to Tanglewood, my twin is perched on the gate waiting. She jumps down and runs along the lane towards me, fair hair fluttering out in the breeze.

'What is it?' she wants to know. 'What happened? Something did, I know! Something good?'

It doesn't happen as much as it used to, but Skye and I can still pick up on each other's thoughts and feelings. It happened back in February when Skye was sick with flu and wandered off from our birthday party and passed out in the woods, in the snow . . . I could feel her, slipping away from me, and somehow I knew just where to look. Skye reckons I saved her life that night. I don't know about that. I am pretty sure we'd have found her one way or another.

Now it is happening again.

'Is it . . . something to do with the film crew and the movie they're making here this summer?' Skye asks. 'Has the ballet school been asked to provide extras? That would be awesome!'

That bursts my bubble.

'Nothing to do with the film,' I say.

Ever since we heard that a film crew was descending on Tanglewood to make a movie this summer, we've talked about the possibility of getting bit parts, but now I know Mum and Paddy will be away while it's happening I'm not so keen. I'm worried the film crew will take over the house, turn everything upside down . . . and that things will just descend into chaos without Mum around.

I am not at all keen on chaos, as you might have noticed.

'Something to do with dancing then?' Skye guesses. 'Tell me, Summer, please!'

'I've been asked to audition for a new dance school,' I say, and even as I speak, I realize I can't quite believe it yet. 'A specialist boarding school, Skye. It's a scholarship place, so it wouldn't cost a fortune, and the principal is Sylvie Rochelle, the French ballerina from that poster I have of *The Firebird*! She picked me out, and Jodie, and a senior girl called Sushila . . . she wants us to apply. Can you believe it?'

'Of course,' Skye says. 'You're brilliant, Summer, don't you know that? My super-talented sister!'

'It's an audition, not an actual place,' I point out. 'I'll have to work like crazy if I'm going to stand any kind of a chance . . .'

'You always work like crazy,' Skye shrugs. 'You'll do it, I know you will!'

You didn't last time, the voice of doubt inside my head points out, and panic unfurls inside me. It's a while since I've heard that voice, but I recognize its message loud and clear: it thinks I will fail. I take a deep breath, gritting my teeth. This time, failure is not an option.

On Friday, when Skye, Coco and I get in from school, Mum is sitting at the kitchen table sipping tea and picking through a glossy brochure for Rochelle Academy.

'It arrived today,' she tells me. 'Along with a letter from Miss Elise and a whole heap of forms. It looks terrific, Summer, but it would be a big change, a big commitment. Are you sure this is what you want?'

You might as well ask me if I want air to breathe.

'I'm sure,' I say. 'Don't you see, Mum? I thought I'd blown my chances of a career in dance, but maybe I can still do it! Maybe it's not just a dream!'

'I've always said you can do anything you set your mind to,' Mum says. 'You're choosing a difficult path, though, Summer. I want to be sure you've thought it through.'

I have thought of little else since I met Sylvie Rochelle. I have thought of little else since forever.

'I have,' I tell Mum.

'Well then,' she sighs. 'Paddy and I will support you in any way we can. You have a talent, Summer, we've always known that. Of course you must go.'

I flop down into a seat beside Mum, biting my lip. 'It's just an audition,' I remind her. 'There are only three places left, and people are applying from all around the country. I might not get in. Lots of people don't make the grade.'

'You will,' Skye says matter-of-factly. 'I know you will.'

I wish I was half as sure.

'It looks awesome,' she continues, leafing through the brochure. 'A real old country house. So pretty.'

❀❀❀❀❀❀❀❀❀❀❀❀❀❀❀❀❀❀❀❀❀

'I am so jealous!' Coco comments. 'Boarding school! Like Hogwarts! How cool?'

'It's cool,' I agree. 'But I don't think it'll be like Hogwarts. It'll be more leotards and leg warmers than Potions lessons and invisibility cloaks . . .'

I study the glossy photographs, the schedules of morning lessons and afternoon dance. I look at the line-up of dance teachers, most of them ex-professionals, and I wonder if I will ever actually be there, dancing in the shiny new studio, living the dream. My stomach twists with doubt.

'There's just one snag,' Mum says. 'According to the letter, your audition is in the middle of August . . . while Paddy and I are away on honeymoon. I'd have liked to be there with you, look around, talk to this Sylvie Rochelle. I want to be sure it's the right place for you.'

'Oh . . . you'll still be away?' I frown.

'Your audition is on the Saturday morning – we're home the following day,' Mum says. 'Bad timing, but we can't change it. Perhaps if we called the dance school and tried to postpone the audition . . .'

'No, don't do that,' I say, panicking. 'There'll be lots of

people trying out for this. I'll go on the official day – I don't want special treatment.'

I like to stick to the rules – I don't want those rules to be bent for me. That might seem childish, unprofessional. What if Sylvie Rochelle thought I wasn't committed enough, that I was too scared to dance without my mum there?

I dredge up a smile. 'Mum, it's not a problem,' I insist. 'There'll be time to look around if I actually get a place. Miss Elise can take me, and Jodie and Sushila will be there.'

Mum sighs. 'I know, I know. But . . . are you sure you'll be OK on your own?'

She doesn't say it out loud, but I know what she's thinking . . . *After last time?*

Well, yeah. Last time, when Dad was in charge and I arrived late and flustered and let the chance of a place at the Royal Ballet School slip through my fingers.

It was my own fault, of course. I should have known Dad would be too preoccupied with his own life to put me first, but back then I still thought I could fix everything, glue our broken family back together. I wanted Dad to see me dance, to be proud of me, to love me so much he'd change his mind about the divorce.

❀❀❀❀❀❀❀❀❀❀❀❀❀❀❀❀❀❀❀❀

It didn't quite work out that way. I fell to pieces right in front of him, and I saw the look in his eyes, although he tried to hide it. I saw his disappointment, his pity, his irritation. I wasn't good enough, not for the Royal Ballet School and not for Dad.

Maybe if I can prove myself this time, I'll finally achieve my dream – and my dad's respect, his pride, his love.

Mum puts an arm round my shoulders, pulling me close.

'You can do it, Summer,' she tells me. 'And whether I'm there to watch you or not, I promise I'll be rooting for you every inch of the way.'

7

'You're kidding me, right?' Aaron says when I tell him about the audition. 'Boarding school? Seriously?'

His arm round my shoulder feels heavy, oppressive, and I shake him off like an unwanted jacket on a warm evening. We are walking along the beach at Kitnor, watching the sun sink slowly into the slate-blue ocean. It should be romantic, but it isn't – I just feel irritated now. I didn't expect Aaron to understand, not really – but I thought he might at least be pleased for me.

'Don't you get it?' I ask. 'This is important. Opportunities like this don't come along every day! Just once or twice in a lifetime, maybe . . .'

Aaron shakes his head. 'No, I really don't get it,' he

says. 'So you're into dancing. So what? Why can't you wait until you're older and do a dance course at uni or something?'

'It doesn't work like that,' I sigh. 'Not if you want to get to the very top. You have to start young, get the best teachers, really push yourself. To be picked out is a big deal, Aaron. If I get through the audition, I'm going. I have to!'

He rakes a hand through his hair, exasperated. 'You spend all your spare time on ballet as it is. Isn't that enough?'

'No!' I say. 'There's only so far I can go at a local dance school, and I want more. At Rochelle Academy I'd be doing regular lessons in the morning and then dancing all afternoon, with teachers who've been professional dancers in some of the best companies in the world. It'd be way more intense . . .'

'More stressful too,' he persists. 'You're already obsessed with ballet. You're thirteen, Summer, you're supposed to have a life!'

Ballet is my life, I want to say, but the words stick in my throat. I know that's not what Aaron wants to hear.

✿✿✿✿✿✿✿✿✿✿✿✿✿✿✿✿✿✿

'What about us?' he asks at last, his face closed and sulky. *What about us?* I want to snap right back, but I don't, of course.

'We'll be OK,' I tell him. 'We can write, and text, and email. And we'll see each other in the holidays.'

'It won't be the same,' he argues, and I realize that if I go away, there probably won't be letters or texts or emails. Aaron is the kind of boy who likes to have a girlfriend he can hang out with, a girl to take to parties, to walk with, hand in hand, along the beach. A girl who lives a hundred miles away is not a lot of use to him.

With a boy like Aaron, there will always be other girls – girls like Marisa McKenna – waiting in the wings. If I pass the audition, I will lose my boyfriend. The thought doesn't upset me as much as it should.

'I guess we'd better make the most of this summer,' Aaron says, and his arm slides round my waist, pulling me close again. I don't wriggle away this time, and after a while, the sun drops lower, painting the sky with washes of crimson and mauve. It's chilly now.

Aaron kisses me, and I try to lose myself in the kiss the way I lose myself in dancing sometimes, but it doesn't

❀❀❀❀❀❀❀❀❀❀❀❀❀❀❀❀❀❀❀❀❀

work. I find myself thinking about the way my boyfriend's arms, wrapped tight around me, feel like a prison.

When I get to dance class next day, Jodie is there wearing a new pair of pointe shoes and one of the burgundy leotards reserved for the senior class. 'Miss Elise thinks I'm ready,' she says, her eyes shining. 'She says if I work hard, I can try just a little pointe work in the audition. It won't matter that I'm inexperienced, she says. They're looking for potential, not the finished product.'

'You're going for it then?' I ask.

'We have to, don't we?' Jodie shrugs. 'We'd be crazy not to try.'

'Do you think we have a chance?'

Jodie grins. 'As good a chance as anyone,' she says.

In class, I watch Jodie take her first few halting steps en pointe, and I can see that although she looks a little awkward and uncomfortable now, there is a grace there, a vibrancy. This audition is a second chance for Jodie too – will Sylvie Rochelle judge her body or her dancing? Will it matter that she is 'the wrong shape' for ballet?

Miss Elise is taking no chances. She asks Jodie, Sushila

and I to sign up for a series of private lessons to prepare for the auditions. 'No charge,' she says, glancing at me. 'If you like, you can help out in the summer sessions in return.'

'I'll help, definitely,' I promise. 'That'd be fun.'

'I might too,' Jodie agrees. 'Cool.'

'Lovely,' Miss Elise says. 'The thing is, I want you to be prepared for this, all three of you. They'll want to see some barre exercises, a set piece – I can help you prepare that – and they're asking for an expressive dance too. You'll each need to choose a piece of music that really inspires you and choreograph a dance to fit it . . .'

I bite my lip, nodding. Already I am scanning through the ballets I know, shortlisting music. I like a challenge.

'Give it your best shot,' Miss Elise says. 'It would be a credit to us here if one of you got a scholarship place with Sylvie.'

One of us. There are three places up for grabs, but of course dozens of girls will be trying out for those places. Miss Elise thinks I am good, but am I good enough? Anxiety flutters inside my belly like birds' wings beating against glass. Not to be chosen . . . that would feel like the end of the world. But who says I am any better than Jodie, with her grace, her energy? Or Sushila, who has been in the senior class a whole eighteen months longer than me and took the lead role of Cinderella in the Christmas dance show?

'Time for a smoothie?' Jodie asks me after class, as we push through the double doors and out into the June sunshine. 'Before you catch your bus?'

'Sure,' I say. 'Why not?'

We go to a cafe down on the seafront, order smoothies and slices of cake and sit in a window seat.

'I am so excited about this audition,' Jodie says. 'I never thought I'd get a second chance at full-time ballet school. Mum thinks I shouldn't build my hopes up, especially after last time, but I can't help it, Summer. I want this so much!'

'Me too,' I sigh, spearing a forkful of carrot cake. 'At least we've experienced a big audition. We know what to expect.'

'That's the trouble,' Jodie says. 'Last time – well, it seemed to go so well. They liked my dancing, I know they did. And then . . . all that stuff about body types and dancers. It was horrible. I felt so useless. But you have to develop a thick skin in this business, Summer. You have to keep trying. You can't give up!'

'Not ever,' I agree, but I am not sure if I have a thick

skin, not at all. The tiniest criticism or put-down soaks into me and lies in my heart like a stone. Sometimes that spurs me on to work harder, but sometimes it just fills me up with sadness.

'We can learn from last time,' I muse. 'I did everything wrong . . . it was just after Dad left and we were late, and . . . well, I wasn't really prepared. This time, I will be. This time, it'll be different.'

'I hope so,' Jodie says. 'Mum said I had a bit of puppy fat back then, but that I've grown into my figure now. She says hourglass shapes are back in vogue these days!'

'Right,' I say, but I'm not too sure if hourglass figures will ever be in vogue when it comes to ballet. All the famous dancers I have ever seen have been small, slender, strong. They have slim, willowy figures. Doesn't Jodie know that?

I watch her bite into a slice of chocolate cake with thick buttercream icing, and I decide that she really doesn't. You wouldn't eat chocolate cake if you were worried about your shape, would you?

Or carrot cake, the voice inside my head points out.

My cheeks flood with heat. Jodie is not the only one with curves these days. The cake turns to sawdust in my mouth.

55

Carrot cake sounds healthy, but I bet it's still full of fat and sugar, and that's the last thing I need right now. Jodie may not be picking up the clues about dancers needing a long, lean shape, but I am. I won't allow my own curves to get in the way of a chance to shine. I push my plate away with a twinge of regret, the cake half eaten.

8

Skye barges into our bedroom right in the middle of my ballet practice, her face lit up.

'They're here!' she announces, straw hat askew, blue eyes flashing. 'The film crew is here! Come on, Summer, let's go see!'

'I'm practising!' I argue.

'So what?' Skye huffs. 'You can do that any time . . . but it's not every day a film crew comes to the village! Aren't you interested? Don't you care? Come on!'

I am not interested, not really . . . I have enough on my plate right now and the film is one crazy complication I could do without. Skye feels differently, though, and reluctantly I allow myself to be dragged away, across the garden and down to JJ's dad's field where a convoy of trailers and makeshift studios have suddenly appeared.

It looks like a circus has come to town. There is a canteen and kitchen trailer, a make-up truck and a whole bunch of caravans and marquees. A couple of gypsy caravans, like the one in our garden, are parked up on the grass. Filming isn't due to start for another week so only a skeleton crew is here, yet already the place is buzzing with life. A woman is ironing old-fashioned dresses in the costume tent, and two teenage boys are painting scenery that looks like vintage fairground signs. Electricity and water have been laid on and there are Portaloos and showers too. Music drifts through the hazy afternoon sunshine and an aroma of curry is wafting from the kitchen trailer.

'It's like a festival,' Skye breathes. 'We'll get to see it all – and some of the production team will actually be staying with us!'

The leading actors will be dotted about the village in holiday cottages, but the producer, director and a bunch of others who need reliable Internet and phone lines will be based at Tanglewood all summer, in the rooms we usually rent out to B&B guests. It's yet another thing I could do without.

'It's going to be weird,' I frown. 'Mum and Paddy away and a big-shot TV producer staying . . .'

'Nikki, she's called,' Skye reminds me. 'The producer. The one who came to stay in the spring, when she was sussing out locations . . .'

'That's right . . . the one with the good-looking son,' I remember. 'What was his name again?'

'Jamie Finch,' Skye says, her cheeks flooding with pink. 'His friends call him Finch apparently . . .'

I look at Skye, picking up on her blush, her eager tone. I remember her questions a few days back about what it feels like to fall in love, and the penny finally drops. My twin is crushing on a boy called Jamie Finch, a boy who will be spending the summer at Tanglewood. The clues were there when Jamie and his mum were here, back in the spring . . . I guess I just didn't take the time to notice them. Back then I was worried that my twin and I were drifting apart, and although we're working on that now, I can see there's still lots we don't know about each other. I promise myself we'll stay close this summer, be there for each other.

'So . . . you think he's good-looking then?' Skye is asking. 'Jamie?'

'Well, you obviously do,' I grin. 'Honestly, Skye, I don't know why I didn't pick up on it sooner. You couldn't take your eyes off him when he was here. And I bet he likes you too – face it, he'd be crazy not to!'

Skye laughs. 'I don't suppose he even noticed me, not that way, but . . . well, I noticed him. D'you think he might like me, Summer? Honestly? I mean, you know these things. You've got Aaron . . .'

My smile slips a little and I haul it back into place before Skye can notice. Yes, I have Aaron, but I sometimes wish I didn't. Dating one of the popular boys from school used to feel cool, but lately, it is starting to feel slightly oppressive. Dates with Aaron are a tangle of anxiety about saying the right thing, or finding anything to say at all. I have to remember to look interested when he tells me about his latest Xbox game or the footy match he watched at the weekend. I have to pretend to look interested when he leans in to kiss me.

I am not quite as expert as Skye thinks when it comes to boys.

'Jamie Finch likes you,' I tell Skye, hoping I'm right.

'Maybe,' Skye sighs. 'I don't suppose I'll even see him, most of the time . . .'

✿✿✿✿✿✿✿✿✿✿✿✿✿✿✿✿✿✿✿✿✿✿

'Of course you'll see him!' I tell her. 'He'll be living in the house with us, won't he? With the production crew. Your eyes will meet over the breakfast table across a plate of Grandma Kate's French toast, and violins will start playing in the background . . .'

'If this is a fantasy, can we leave Coco and her music practice out of it?' my twin protests. 'Please. No cats-being-strangled!' She elbows me in the ribs and I slide off the wall, dragging her with me. We fall into each other, laughing, and the set painters stop their work to peer at us, slightly perplexed.

'Shhh!' I whisper. 'They'll think we're mad!'

'So what? We are,' Skye giggles, and the set painters wave and abandon their brushes, walking over to talk to us. Their names are Chris and Marty and it turns out that they are theatre design students helping on the film for the summer. We tell them we're from Tanglewood House and they seem to know all about us . . . the B&B where the production bosses will be staying and the chocolate workshop and the five stepsisters.

'We're filming your gypsy caravan too,' Marty grins. 'Bringing it down to the woods along with the two we have

61

here. Great location. This must be an awesome place to live.'

'It's OK,' I shrug.

And then I think of the beach and the ocean and the woods with their little twisty trees; I think of the moss-green fields, the hills, the moors, the village with its jigsaw of thatched cottages and old-fashioned shops crowded together. I would miss all of that if – when – I go away to dance school.

Chris and Marty give us a guided tour of the camp. We get to see the props tent and the hair and make-up truck with its mirrors and swivel chairs, its palettes of colour and pots of lipstick, its hairdryers, straighteners and curling tongs. The minute we step into the wardrobe tent Skye is lost, transfixed by the racks of embroidered dresses and faded tweed jackets.

'It's like the best and biggest vintage shop ever,' she breathes, and Jess the wardrobe manager laughs and stops her ironing to show us the clothes. A few minutes later we are twirling around in fringy shawls, feet clomping in pairs of ancient buttoned boots. When the dresses are safely back on their hangers, Chris breaks open a couple of cans of

Coke. I take one without thinking, letting the sweet, dark fizz explode on my tongue.

'I'll have an assistant from next week,' Jess is telling us. 'But I can always use an extra pair of hands, if either of you are interested? Wardrobe can get crazy with period dramas like this one. We've a couple of big crowd scenes with extras in, and they're always total madness. It wouldn't be glamorous, just ironing, mending, helping the actors and actresses . . .'

'I'm interested,' Skye answers, her eyes shining. 'I've never been more interested in anything in my whole, entire life! I'd love to help!'

'OK,' Jess grins. 'Brilliant! You too, Summer, if you like?'

I say nothing. A few weeks of hanging out with the film crew, helping with the costumes while a film is shot practically in our own backyard . . . it sounds too good to be true, and of course it is.

I know that my August will not be spent here, helping out in the costume tent, watching the filming unfold. It will be spent in the studios of the Exmoor School of Dance, practising, pushing, striving for perfection, preparing for my audition. I have a dream to pin down, and that dream has nothing at all to do with films or fun or summer jobs.

❀❀❀❀❀❀❀❀❀❀❀❀❀❀❀❀❀❀❀❀❀❀

You have to make sacrifices, Miss Elise says, to get to the top in ballet, and if that means missing out on some of the fun this summer, well, fine. The dream means more to me.

'Maybe,' I shrug, but there is no maybe about it. I won't be helping out. I can't afford the time, the distraction, not even for something like this. Suddenly, the Coke tastes sickly – nothing but sugar and bubbles and empty calories.

Skye chats on, telling Jess about her collection of 1920s velvet dresses and cloche hats. Me, I put the can down and step back, on to the edge of things, into the background.

9

I am standing at the salad bar in the school canteen, trying to decide whether I can face yet another plate of lettuce, tomatoes and sweetcorn or whether I could cut loose a bit and have tuna pasta. My stomach is growling with hunger.

Alfie, the most annoying boy in the western hemisphere, appears at my elbow.

'Swap you,' he says, wafting his dish of syrup pudding and custard right under my nose. 'Go on . . . sure I can't tempt you?'

The pudding smells gorgeous, but I know it is bad news, the kind of pudding that should carry a government health warning. Death by syrup pudding. At least you'd die happy, I guess.

'Get lost, Alfie,' I sigh. 'Dancers don't eat that kind of stodge.'

'You could eat anything you wanted to, Summer,' he shrugs. 'You're really slim and pretty. And dancing must burn up about a million calories a second anyhow . . .'

Slim and pretty? I look at Alfie and he smiles, his brown eyes holding mine. He's good, I have to admit. He almost has me fooled. A part of me actually thinks he might mean the compliment, and then I remind myself that Alfie lives to wind people up.

'I've been watching you,' he says quietly. 'You've been surviving on rabbit food lately.'

Anger catches in my throat, hot and sharp and sore. Alfie has no right to be watching me, noticing what I choose to eat. I always make healthy choices, but I have made a conscious decision to eat mostly salads lately. I can't shift Jodie's words about being told she was the 'wrong' shape for dancing, and I'm determined nobody will ever be able to say that to me. Nothing is going to come between me and my dance school dream.

'Don't watch me then,' I whisper. 'I never asked you to. I mean it, Alfie. I don't need your wisecracks right now.'

'What's up?' Aaron demands, appearing at my side and squeezing my waist as if marking out his territory. 'Is he bugging you, Summer?'

'No more than usual,' I say. 'Alfie didn't want his pudding, so he offered it to me, but . . . I don't want it either. Obviously.'

'She's keeping an eye on her figure,' Aaron says with a grin. 'I'm keeping an eye on it too, and between us we have it covered, Alfie. We don't need your help. Clear off.'

My cheeks burn.

When Aaron first asked me out, I was so flattered I just about fell over myself to accept. These days, he seems to annoy me more every time I see him. When he puts his hands on my waist in the middle of the school canteen and tells the class joker he is watching my figure, I just want to cringe.

Alfie shrugs sadly, hands me the syrup pudding and walks away. The aroma of hot syrup and custard makes my mouth water, but I know it is not the kind of thing my body needs. It would be a bad idea to even taste it. Wouldn't it?

Aaron rolls his eyes, lifts the dish out of my hands and tips the pudding into the bin.

*

❀❀❀❀❀❀❀❀❀❀❀❀❀❀❀❀❀

School is winding down in a muddle of school trips and sports days. Even on ordinary days, the teachers shift down a gear, filling lesson time with quizzes and films. Less homework means more time for dancing, but I'm looking forward to the holidays when I'll have weeks to devote to rehearsing for the audition. My friends are looking forward to summer for different reasons, though.

'This is going to be the best break ever,' Tia says as we loaf on the school playing fields at lunchtime the next day, making daisy chains and trying to soak up some sunshine. My friends are snacking on crisps and doughnuts; I have chosen an apple instead.

I am writing a sneaky rota in the back of my homework diary, planning out the next three weeks. I pencil in regular ballet lessons, dates for our extra sessions, days when the senior studio at the dance school is free. Then I block out time at home to work on my expressive dance and time for general practice.

'We're thirteen years old,' Tia is saying, in between mouthfuls of doughnut. 'Proper teenagers! We should make the most of every minute!'

'Too right,' Millie chips in, nudging Skye and me.

'Especially you two, with no parents keeping an eye on you for three whole weeks – Tanglewood can be party central!'

'No chance,' Skye laughs. 'Our gran is staying to keep an eye on us – we'll have to be on our best behaviour!'

Millie shrugs. 'Grans are pretty soft, right? You can wind them round your little finger usually. Just say you're missing your mum and need to have lots of parties with your friends to take your mind off it all . . .'

'That wouldn't be fair on Grandma Kate,' I say.

I add a list of things I can do to help Grandma Kate to my rota, then frown. My days are looking pretty full. It doesn't leave a lot of time for socializing.

'Come on,' Tia says. 'You have a movie being made right on your doorstep, and a whole bunch of crew camped out in the next field. Not to mention the important ones right there in your house. It's the most exciting thing to happen in Kitnor in ages! You have to have at least a few parties!'

Tia peers over my shoulder trying to see what I'm writing.

'Summer! That looks like the dullest holiday ever!' She grabs the pen out of my hand and writes *FUN* across the page in giant letters, in case I am not getting the message. My neatly drawn rota is wrecked, but I try not to mind.

'We could try to squeeze in the occasional party,' Skye says. 'We'll work on Grandma Kate!'

Tia and Millie and Skye start planning beach bonfires and picnic parties and whether to invite boys from school or try to get to know any cute teen-boy actors taking part in the film. I frown and decide to copy out my rota again, once I get home. Minus the fun. I pick some daisies and thread them together instead.

'There have to be some boys in the film,' Millie frowns. 'It's the law of averages, right? And teen-boy actors are bound to be hot.'

'They'll be better than the local talent anyhow,' Tia comments, watching Alfie and a bunch of other boys running piggyback races across the grass. There is lots of staggering, flailing arms and yelling. 'It's really quite depressing. No offence, Millie . . . I know you like Alfie. He isn't bad-looking, but he's just such a clown!'

Millie and Alfie hooked up at my thirteenth birthday party, although they've avoided each other since. Alfie is polite but distant with Millie, as though the kiss never happened, but I think she still has a bit of a crush going on. There is no accounting for taste.

70

There's a bloodcurdling scream and Sid Sharma charges towards us with Alfie on his back, his mouth stretched wide into a victory yell. Sid gallops into the middle of our group and lets go of Alfie abruptly. He crashes down at our feet, and as he falls, his trousers somehow slither to half mast, revealing a billowing pair of lime-green polka-dot boxers. Sid runs away, laughing, and we howl and cover our eyes.

'Gross!' Tia yelps. 'Pull your trousers up, Alfie!'

'I feel sick,' Millie says. 'Girls, I'm over him. It's official.'

'Sorry!' Alfie grins brightly, wrestling his trousers back up to a respectable level. 'Sid can be a pain sometimes. He thinks he's funny.'

'He's not,' I say crisply. 'And nor are you, Alfie. Scram, OK? We're in the middle of a very serious conversation!'

'I can do serious!' Alfie protests. 'Just go right ahead, girls. Don't mind me. I like political debate, and culture, and . . . um . . . well, whatever. Talk away!'

Millie gives him a withering look and turns her back on him. 'It's a very serious conversation indeed,' she agrees. 'We're discussing the film they're making in the village this summer.'

'Cool,' Alfie says, peering over Millie's shoulder and pulling a sad face at me. 'I'm happy to talk about that . . .'

71

'Ignore him, Millie,' I sigh. 'It's the only way.'

'I am,' she huffs. 'Don't worry. What I was going to say was, d'you think they'll let us actually watch the filming? Because they might pick one of us out of the crowd and give us a part. I might shoot to stardom and end up rich and famous, like Emma Watson or something . . .'

'Don't give up the day job, Millie,' Alfie Anderson quips. 'If I remember rightly, the last time you were in a school play you forgot your lines, tripped over your angel dress and fell right off the stage.'

'I was six years old!' Millie huffs. 'Honestly, Alfie, my acting skills have improved a LOT since then.'

'Maybe,' he shrugs. 'Only . . . if anyone was going to get a bit part in the film, I'd say it would most likely be Summer . . . she's had tons of experience in the spotlight. She'd be brilliant.'

Alfie grins and a familiar panic begins to flutter inside my chest. I hate it when he winds me up. He has been making jokes at my expense ever since I can remember, and even though his words seem innocent enough this time, I'm pretty sure he is laughing at me.

'Not funny, Alfie,' I say.

72

'Wasn't meant to be,' he shrugs. He winks at me and picks up the daisy chain I've been making, slipping it into his pocket before sauntering away. Some boys really are infuriating.

'Definitely no lads from school at our beach parties and picnics,' Millie is saying.

'What about Aaron?' Tia asks on my behalf. 'You can't ban boys!'

I can't help thinking I'd quite like a summer without Aaron, but I feel disloyal. You are not supposed to get bored with your boyfriend this easily, not when they are one of the popular crew.

'Aaron can come, of course,' Millie concedes. 'He's Summer's boyfriend! The cool boys can come . . . but no Alfie Anderson!'

'Alfie's OK,' Skye says kindly. 'He's a mate, yeah?'

'Well,' Tia shrugs. 'Long as he keeps his trousers up.'

Millie sighs. 'You lot are too soft,' she says, but she's smiling, imagining a long, sunny summer of sandy beaches and swimming in the ocean, the excitement of the filming, warm nights filled with driftwood bonfires and guitar music and laughter and kisses.

I can't imagine any of that. When I try to picture it, my mind goes blank, like a computer screen that has crashed and died. I listen to my sister and my friends planning endless treats and fun in the sun, and all I can think of is ballet practice and auditions, of making the dream real. I slip the homework diary with its ruined rota into my school-bag.

There's a low, gnawing ache in my stomach, and I can't tell whether it's anxiety or hunger.

*Girl Most Likely
to Succeed
Summer Tanberry!*

10

It's the last week of term, and Paddy and Mum are preparing for their trip. Our gypsy caravan has been wheeled down to the woods to create one of the film sets, and Paddy has employed a retired teacher from the village to keep the chocolate business running while he is away. Every morning Harry wheezes up to Tanglewood on an ancient bicycle, ready to learn the mysteries of making the perfect truffle. He is cheery and eccentric, with a grey handlebar moustache and a selection of jaunty bow ties.

Paddy gathers us all together to run through the plans. 'Harry will manage the day-to-day running of the chocolate workshop,' he explains. 'Keep things ticking over. There's enough stock in the fridges to last a lifetime so he may not actually need to do anything from scratch, and Grandma

Kate can bank the cheques and keep an eye on the website. It's only three weeks and we haven't put any fresh ads in the press so things shouldn't get too crazy . . .'

'Stop worrying, Paddy,' Harry cuts in. 'You can count on me. The girls will help out if we're snowed under with orders, right, ladies?'

'Right, Harry,' Skye, Cherry and Coco chorus. I nod weakly, but I really hope I'm not needed because I can't see when I'll have the time. I don't have a single idea for my expressive dance and I need to settle on something soon, I know. I'm already doubtful that I'll be able to help out at the summer sessions week at the dance school, even though I promised Miss Elise I would – it's just so close to the audition date.

Honey doesn't share my guilt. She just raises an eyebrow, amused. I am pretty sure Harry won't be getting any help from her while Mum and Paddy are away.

I'm just getting used to Harry mooching about the place when Tanglewood House is invaded. The film production team move in, colonizing the B&B rooms and turning the guest breakfast room into an office. We pass them on the staircase, or see them in the garden tapping away on iPads or laptops in the evening sun. They look cool, creative and scarily busy.

'We'll be self-sufficient really,' Nikki the producer explains, sipping black coffee at the kitchen table. 'We're not expecting cooked breakfasts or daily room tidies. We just want peace and quiet to work, good Wi-Fi and landline phones and a place to get away from the film sets sometimes.'

'We can certainly manage that,' Mum assures her. 'There'll be cereal, bread, jam and a toaster in the breakfast room, along with a microwave and a small fridge stocked up with milk, fruit and juice. If you need anything else, just ask.'

'We won't be any trouble, I promise,' Nikki replies. 'Although I suspect Jamie might like some teenage company when he's not working . . . he'll be here on Saturday, once school finishes.'

'The girls will sort that out,' Mum promises. 'Right?'

'Right,' I say. 'We'll introduce him to our friends, make sure he doesn't feel left out. Won't we, Skye?'

'Definitely,' my twin whispers.

Nobody but me notices her blush.

*

❀❀❀❀❀❀❀❀❀❀❀❀❀❀❀❀❀❀❀❀❀❀

Friday is the last day of term, the last day ever at Exmoor Park Middle School for me and Skye. There's a leavers' assembly with Mum and Paddy and everyone else's parents squished on to plastic chairs, dabbing their eyes with tissues and looking proud. I remember when Dad used to come to things like this, school plays and carol concerts and parents' evenings, back when we were at primary. Well, he came once or twice.

Some of the boys have formed a band and play a song about reaching for the stars, Tia reads a poem about always doing your best and there's a slideshow of photos to watch. There we all are in kayaks; at a science fair; on the Year Seven trip to Alton Towers; in a school production of *Bugsy Malone* (I was Tallulah, and I loved the dance scenes – of course).

It's weird to see how we have changed from bright-eyed nine-year-olds in shiny new school uniform into proper teenagers, reliant on hair gel and straighteners and eyeliner. We have outgrown middle school now. We don't talk about dolls and ponies these days, we talk about boy bands and make-up and who fancies who.

We laugh and chew gum and touch up our lipgloss in the

78

corridor between classes, but I wonder how many of us wish we could be nine again, go back to simpler times when we didn't have to worry about bras or periods or boys, when it was still OK to play make-believe games or eat a chocolate bar without thinking about the calories. Sometimes I think that being a teenager is an act, a role we have to take in a play where nobody bothered to show us the script. We scoosh on bodyspray that smells of strawberries, admire the same bands and pretend to be more grown-up than we really are.

We hope that nobody can see through the act. They might see that we're not as confident as we look, that behind the eyeliner and the easy laughs we are actually kind of lost. Or is that just me? It's all such hard work – keeping up appearances especially.

Tia jabs me in the ribs and I snap to attention as the Head begins giving out the end-of-term awards. Everybody gets something. There are awards for the 'brightest smile', the 'wackiest hair', the 'cheekiest grin' and the 'cheesiest jokes'. Yes, that last one goes to Alfie Anderson. Tia gets an award for being a genius at maths, Millie for being good at netball, Skye for having 'the most original sense of style'. Aaron gets the 'sports star' award for being brilliant at footy and I get 'girl most likely to succeed', and everyone claps and cheers and tells us what a great couple we make.

I smile and smile until my face aches.

Later, when the afternoon has crumbled into good-natured disorder, we sign our names on each other's shirts in felt-tip pen, hug and promise to stay in touch forever. For most people, that won't be so difficult. Most of my classmates are moving right up to the high school, but this is not just my last day at Exmoor Park Middle School; it could be my last day of ordinary school ever.

I hold my award tightly, a laminated sheet of A4 that feels like a promise. Does it mean I will succeed at my audition? I hope so.

What if you don't? the voice in my head asks nastily. *What then?*

I push the thought away. You cannot let the mask slip, not when you are the 'girl most likely to succeed'.

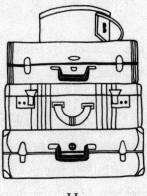

11

When we get home from school that afternoon, Grandma
Kate is there, sweeping through the house like a small
whirlwind. She rolls up her sleeves and chases Mum from
the kitchen, telling her to run a bath, relax, get into honeymoon mode.

Mum and Paddy are in the living room checking passports and travel documents, finishing their packing,
modelling ancient sun hats and dodgy sandals. Their
minds are already several thousand miles away from here,
in the Peruvian rainforest, dreaming of organic, fairly
traded cocoa beans and llamas and the Lost City of the
Incas.

'Be good for Grandma Kate,' Mum says, her face creased
into a frown. 'Try not to be any trouble, and help make

sure everything runs smoothly. Be friendly. Be helpful. And whatever you do, don't forget the room-changes on Saturdays . . .'

'Mum, we won't,' I promise. 'It's all sorted – I've made a list so everyone knows when to help. It'll run like clock-work!'

'Your curfew is eleven, so no later than that, promise?'

'We promise,' we chorus, except for Honey who is suddenly busy checking her phone.

'Honey?' Mum prompts.

My big sister looks up sulkily. 'Eleven?' she asks. 'Seriously? I'm fifteen, not five!'

Mum stops packing and turns to Honey, hands on hips. 'We agreed, Honey,' she says. 'Eleven. The last thing I want is Grandma Kate worrying about where you are. If you can't go along with that, the whole thing's off.'

Silence falls around us, and Paddy rakes a hand through his hair, despairing. Honey breaks the silence.

'OK, OK,' she laughs. 'Don't panic, it was a joke, yeah? I will stick to the curfew. I promise.'

Mum relaxes, and Paddy's shoulders slump in relief. 'Harry knows what he's doing in the chocolate workshop,' he says. 'He should keep that side of things ticking over nicely, but if there are any problems . . .'

'There won't be,' Skye promises.

'It's all under control,' Grandma Kate tells Mum and Paddy. 'Stop worrying! The girls and I will manage just fine, and Harry will run the workshop with military precision. All you two have to do is go off and enjoy yourselves!'

'But three weeks . . .' Mum sighs. 'I don't know. Anything could go wrong . . .'

'Nothing will,' I promise, but there's a sad, empty ache in my chest that tells me things are going wrong right now. I want to hang on to Mum and hug her hard and beg her not to go, but I don't, of course. That would be childish and selfish and cruel. Wouldn't it?

'Summer, I so wish I could be here for your audition,' Mum is saying. 'I know how much it means to you. I'll be thinking of you, wishing you luck every inch of the way. I'll text whenever I can, I promise.'

'It's OK.' I drag up my best stage smile, think bright, happy thoughts. Let's just say that if my dancing career falls through, I could have a great future in acting.

❀❀❀❀❀❀❀❀❀❀❀❀❀❀❀❀❀❀

Mum squeezes my hand and I have to turn away, tears prickling the back of my eyes without warning.

Next morning, we are up at dawn to say goodbye. The suitcases have been packed into Paddy's minivan and Mum is frantically looking around in case she's forgotten anything. 'You'll walk Fred and feed the ducks, won't you, Coco?' she asks. 'And make sure Humbug is shut safely in the stable every night?'

'You can rely on me,' Coco promises.

'Call me if there are any problems,' Mum says. 'I'll have my mobile switched on at all times, in case of emergencies . . .'

'There won't be any emergencies,' Grandma Kate says firmly, but Mum doesn't seem to be listening.

'There's lentil soup, home-made steak pie and sausage casserole in the freezer,' she says. 'Remember not to overstack the dishwasher. Keep an eye on The Chocolate Box website and log orders as they come in . . . bank the business payments at least once a week . . . water the veggie garden . . .'

'Relax, Charlotte,' Grandma Kate says gently. 'Time to switch off, enjoy the honeymoon.'

❀❀❀❀❀❀❀❀❀❀❀❀❀❀❀❀❀❀❀❀❀❀❀

Mum hugs us all hard, and Paddy tousles our hair as if we are bouncy puppy dogs and not soon-to-be-abandoned children. They jump in the car and Paddy revs the engine while Mum leans out of the open window. 'Do everything Grandma Kate tells you . . . and stick to the curfew, OK?'

They drive away fast in a screech of gravel.

'We'll cope just fine,' Grandma Kate says briskly, turning back towards the house. 'Let's hope they have the best honeymoon ever. Now . . . let's get this show on the road! Who'd like some of my special French toast for breakfast?'

'Me,' Coco whoops.

'Me too,' Skye echoes, hooking an arm round Cherry's shoulders. 'Can we have that every morning? It's my favourite! If you've never had my gran's French toast, Cherry, you have not lived. It has cinnamon and butter and a drizzle of maple syrup . . . gorgeous.'

'Cool,' Cherry says.

A few weeks ago I'd have thought it was cool too, but now I am just vaguely irritated that a high-calorie breakfast is meant to make me feel better about Mum going away. My stomach growls with hunger, but I am getting to like that empty feeling. It makes me feel light, clean, strong.

❀❀❀❀❀❀❀❀❀❀❀❀❀❀❀❀❀❀❀❀❀

The others troop back into the house. Honey yawns and says we must be crazy to even think about eating when it's practically the middle of the night, and that she is going back to bed, possibly until lunchtime.

I am left alone, standing on the empty driveway, staring into the distance long after the car has gone.

12

I am in the studio at the dance school, running through my exercises and working on the set piece we have to perform for the audition. The clock on the wall says I have been practising for two hours, but I'm not happy yet with the way it's going.

I need it to be smooth, light, effortless, but today it's not working. I feel dull, leaden, lost. I need the music to fill me up and take me away from this place, somewhere timeless, magical, where dance is the only thing that matters.

I look towards the window. A plane cuts through the cloudless sky, leaving a soft, white surf-like trail in its wake. Are Mum and Paddy on that plane? I have no way of knowing.

All morning my mobile has been buzzing with messages

from Mum. **Almost at Heathrow**, she texted while I was on the bus to town: **Checked in, all well**, as I was getting changed; **Through security**, as I bent to reset the CD; **At the departure gate**, as I stopped to re-dip my shoes in the rosin box; and, finally, for the last twenty minutes, silence.

Mum and Paddy will be in the air right now, heading for Peru, maybe on the plane I glimpsed, or on another plane like it, far away. I am happy for them, so pleased they are getting the honeymoon they deserve . . . but I can't help feeling anxious too.

I can't remember being away from Mum for more than a couple of nights before, on sleepovers or rare, long-ago trips to London to see Dad, or that weekend Mum spent in Glasgow when she was first seeing Paddy. There was a school trip to Wales the year Dad left, an outward-bound type of thing with abseiling and hillwalking, but it seemed wrong to go when Mum was so cut up about the split, when money was short and our family seemed to be falling to pieces. Skye and I binned our application forms without even showing Mum.

I know I'm grown-up enough to manage for a few weeks. It is silly to feel uneasy about it all – we can manage fine, and Grandma Kate is kind and sensible and very organized. It's not like we have been left to fend for ourselves. So I have no idea why worry curdles in my belly like sour milk.

The studio door swings open and Jodie appears, dressed for practice. She seems surprised to see me.

'You're early,' she grins. 'I thought I'd be the first here today!'

I decide not to mention I have been here for two hours already. I've been practising more than usual over the last few weeks, but I don't want to appear too keen, too desperate, too weird.

'Won't it be amazing if we get through those auditions?' Jodie says. 'Come September, we could be at ballet school full-time. I can't stop thinking about it. I'm going to practise every day until the audition.'

'Me too,' I say. 'I'd do anything to get a place, anything at all.'

Jodie frowns. 'Me too,' she says. 'But it's destiny, right? If we're meant to get a place, we will. If not . . . well, it just isn't meant to happen.'

Anger flares inside me. Fate and destiny weren't exactly on my side last time, were they? Surely Jodie isn't willing to leave something as important as this down to fate. Is it enough to dance your best and hope that the panel is feeling kind enough to give you a chance? I don't think so. I think you have to do everything possible to make sure you shine.

'It is meant to happen, though,' I frown. 'It has to. We've wanted this since we were kids, Jodie. If we try hard enough, we'll get through! We have to!'

She shrugs and smiles and starts running through her warm-up exercises, but I get the feeling Jodie thinks I may be trying a little too hard.

She doesn't know the half of it.

At teatime, Jamie Finch arrives at Tanglewood wearing a vintage army jacket and a pair of red Converse, his dark hair a tangle of unruly waves, an outsize rucksack on his back. Nikki drove up to London to collect him, then got ambushed by one of the production team the minute she returned, leaving her son adrift.

He wanders into the kitchen, where we have fruit smoothies and angel-wing meringues waiting. 'Good to meet you, Jamie,' Grandma Kate says. 'Welcome to the madhouse!'

It probably does look a little crazy. Coco is sitting on the draining board playing her violin, which is why Skye is wearing pink fluffy earmuffs as she irons some of her vintage dress collection to take down to Jess the wardrobe manager later. Cherry is curled up in the armchair by the Aga writing haiku poetry and even Honey is sitting at the kitchen table making quick ink sketches of everyone.

I've just unplugged my iPod after running through my ballet exercises one last time, a baggy T-shirt over my leotard and leg warmers. I didn't dance well today in class, and I am determined to smooth out the glitches if it kills me. I am not leaving the audition to fate, no matter what Jodie says.

Fred the dog and Humbug the lamb watch it all, curled up together on Fred's cushion in the corner. We don't always cram into the kitchen together like this, but today is different. We need to be together because Mum and Paddy are gone and everything feels slightly out of balance.

Jamie Finch laughs, taking the chaos in his stride. 'Thank you for having me,' he says politely. 'I'm so excited to be out of London for a while – Mum's never let me help out on a shoot before. It's going to be cool! By the way, just call me Finch . . . everyone else does.'

'Finch then,' Grandma Kate amends.

Coco puts down her violin, blinking, and Honey raises one perfect eyebrow at the idea of a boy who thinks that Kitnor might be cooler than London. I glance across at Skye. She has been counting off the days until Finch's arrival, yet now looks totally amazed to find him standing in the middle of our kitchen.

'Hey,' he says when he catches sight of her. 'Skye . . . how's it going?'

My twin blushes a dark shade of pink and seems to have lost the power of speech. She may not actually have heard his words, what with the pink fluffy earmuffs, but she takes them off carefully now and drops them carelessly into the fruit bowl where they nestle alongside a nectarine and three green apples. She grins and Finch grins back, and when the rest of us notice a faint smell of burning, it's hard to tell for sure whether it comes from their sizzling gaze or from the iron Skye has abandoned face down on one of her best vintage petticoats.

'Skye, be careful!' Grandma Kate says, unplugging the iron and holding up the ruined petticoat, which now has an iron-shaped scorch mark right in the middle.

But Skye can't take her eyes off Finch, not even to survey the frazzled slip. He is just as smitten. It's like watching one of those cheesy movies where everything goes slo-mo and soft focus and your toes begin to curl with embarrassment. I have always thought those scenes were exaggerated because it's seriously not that way at all when I am with Aaron.

'Hello?' Grandma Kate says, bemused. 'Skye? Better leave that ironing now, pet. Finch, why don't you go and find your mum and tell her there's a nice pot of tea here for her. Then I'll show you to your room, and I'm sure the girls will help you to settle in, make you feel welcome . . .'

'Ah . . . OK.'

Finch finally drags his eyes away from my twin sister, grins sheepishly and lopes off to find Nikki, and Skye snaps out of her trance and looks down at the ruined petticoat, frowning slightly as if she can't quite work out what just happened. I am not sure I know either, even with my trusty twin-telepathy on full alert, but I know that it is major, a life-changing event, a catastrophe even, like an earthquake or a tidal wave.

It doesn't take a genius to figure it out. My twin sister is nuts about Jamie Finch, and he seems to feel the same way about her. I'm pleased for her, truly I am, but I cannot shake the feeling that life as we know it will never be the same again.

I bite my lip so hard I taste blood.

13

Tia and Millie burst into our kitchen on Monday morning brandishing a flyer that invites interested locals to earn £50 by appearing as extras in a couple of crowd scenes in the film.

'We could be famous!' Millie declares, eyes wide. 'We could shoot to stardom and end up winning Oscars and strutting down the red carpet with Robert Pattinson!'

'Get a grip,' I say. 'Robert Pattinson isn't even in this film!'

'No, but that bloke from *Hollyoaks* is,' Tia points out. 'And he's quite hot, in a non-sparkly kind of way. Millie's right, we have to do it. They're not auditioning or anything. We just turn up on Saturday for costume fittings. Awesome!'

'Awesome indeed,' Skye says. 'I'll be helping with the

costumes, so I can make sure you get a cool hat or a parasol. Finch says it should be a lot of fun.'

'Oh, well, if Finch says so,' I tease, but it comes out a little snippier than I mean it to. I don't think Skye notices, though. Nothing seems to burst her bubble these last few days.

I have to admit that being an extra might be cool. It's not every summer a movie gets shot right in your backyard, but right now, I don't have time to think about teen-boy actors or dressing up for some retro-themed movie. I am focused on pliés and jetés, and today I have promised myself a whole day in the studio to work on my expressive dance for the audition. I sling my ballet bag over my shoulder and stand up.

'Where are you going?' Skye asks. 'You don't have ballet lessons today!'

'No, but I want to use the studio to practise,' I say. 'I have to go through possible music clips, come up with something for my expressive dance. Something good.'

'But . . . we're going to the beach!' Tia argues. 'It's the first Monday of the holidays . . . we were going to celebrate, hang out and swim and sunbathe! I told Aaron,

96

and everything! He's got a footy match, but he said he'd definitely come down afterwards. You have to stay, Summer! Relax a little!'

I bite back my annoyance. This is the FUN Tia asked me to schedule in this holiday, but I don't have time for it. My priorities for the next few weeks are all about dance; chilling out in the sun and dressing up in straw hats to help fill out the crowd scenes in a film just do not figure. And what's with inviting Aaron? Seriously, that's all I need.

'Summer?' Millie says, cajoling. 'C'mon. You know you want to.'

'I'm busy,' I snap. 'Too busy for swimming and sunbathing. Sorry.' I swing out of the kitchen, letting the door slam shut behind me.

It's only once I'm at the dance school that the churny feeling in my stomach begins to subside. It's stress, I tell myself. Stress about the audition, stress about my expressive dance, stress about Mum and Paddy being on the other side of the planet.

And hunger maybe because today I am running on Coke Zero and indignation. Food, like fun, has been sidelined.

I can't expect Tia and Millie to understand, of course,

❀❀❀❀❀❀❀❀❀❀❀❀❀❀❀❀❀❀❀❀❀❀

and I can see that Skye has other things on her mind right now. I'll apologize to them, tell them I'm under a lot of pressure, maybe go along with them on Saturday to the film thing.

Fun . . . I guess I can try to make room for it on my rota. Just not today.

Miss Elise is surprised to see me, but when I explain that I want to work on my expressive dance, she hands me a box of ballet and classical CDs to look through.

'You should find something there,' she tells me. 'If you choose the right piece of music, the rest should fall into place. This is the one piece I can't really help you with, but it's probably the most important part of your audition because it will tell Sylvie something about you. Good luck, Summer!'

I go upstairs to change, then pull on a loose T-shirt and pad through to the studio. I run through my barre exercises and my pointe work, then sit down beside the little CD player, flicking through Miss Elise's CDs in search of inspiration. It doesn't come. After a while, the music begins to blend into one, endlessly light and bright and airy. I bite my lip. I need something different – something dramatic, powerful, strong.

I remember the poster on my bedroom wall, of Sylvie Rochelle as the Firebird, and scan through the CDs until I find Stravinsky's soundtrack to the ballet. This is better – vivid, energetic, exciting. I skip through the CD until I come to a section that makes my heart beat faster . . . a crazy, chaotic crescendo of sound. I do not like chaos usually, but this music fills me up like oxygen. It feels right.

Checking the cover notes, I see that I've chosen something called the 'Infernal Dance' – a frenzied dance which the Firebird curses the evil wizard's creatures to perform. I listen to it again, smiling. The expressive dance segment of my audition should be my strong point. I love putting sequences together, interpreting music, and now that I have found the right piece of music perhaps I can do that. It's a challenging piece, but Sylvie Rochelle will like that, I know.

All afternoon I try out steps and turns, but nothing seems quite right. I keep trying all the same. I dance until my muscles ache, until my stomach growls with hunger and my toes feel bruised and blistered.

I dance to the point of pain and beyond, as if punishing myself will make everything fall into place.

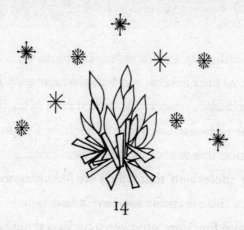

14

I check my mobile on the late bus home, and find four missed calls and eleven unread messages. One message is from Mum, who reports that she and Paddy are now in Lima, the Peruvian capital. The others are from Skye, Millie, Tia and Aaron, informing me that their lazy day at the beach has snowballed into a full-on bonfire party, and to get myself down there pronto.

I groan. By the time I get down to the beach the sun is starting to dip down in the sky and the party is in full swing.

'Finally!' Aaron yells as I approach. 'I thought you'd never get here!'

'Sorry,' I say. 'I lost track of time, you know how it is . . .'

His arm snakes round my waist as I survey the party. Shay Fletcher is playing guitar, Cherry at his side; Coco is toasting marshmallows and Honey is holding court to JJ, Chris and Marty. Tia, Millie, Sid, Carl and Alfie wave and shout hellos at me, but I'm looking for my twin, and I can't see her anywhere.

'Where's Skye?'

'Over there with that Finch kid,' Aaron says. 'Slush central . . . boy, do those two have it bad.'

Skye and Finch are sitting on a driftwood log behind the bonfire, so close they are almost touching. They must be exchanging life stories or something because they are talking non-stop. I don't think they'd notice or care if the rest of us just tiptoed away and left them to it. I try not to feel hurt that after all her frantic texts, my twin hasn't even noticed that I'm here.

Aaron is in the middle of an endless account of some five-a-side footy match he played earlier. My mouth has frozen into a rictus smile, and my ears are starting to feel numb around the edges. Without warning, he leans in to nuzzle my neck, his breath hot and sticky, like Fred when he is snuffling around for a treat. I wish he actually was Fred because then I might not feel quite so alarmed. 'Don't, Aaron,' I hiss. 'People are looking!'

✿✿✿✿✿✿✿✿✿✿✿✿✿✿✿✿✿✿✿✿

'So?' he shrugs. 'You're my girlfriend. It's allowed.'

I pull away, embarrassed, and Aaron scowls. 'You're no fun, Summer,' he huffs. 'You're so . . . uptight lately. All you think about is ballet and that stupid audition!'

'That's not true!' I argue, but Aaron has a point. When we first started going out, I was flattered to have such a cute boyfriend. I loved the silk flower he left in my locker, 'from a secret admirer'. I thought that dating Aaron would be full of things like that, sweet, romantic things, but he never even mentions the flower. I think it was just a tactic, a means to an end.

I fell in love with a boy who left secret presents in my locker and ended up with a boy who talks about football and Xbox games. I wanted romance and I got wet kisses and hands that try to stray to places I don't want them to.

Across the flames of the bonfire, Alfie is watching me, his face thoughtful. There is just no escape from that boy.

'Hey, Aaron!' he yells. 'I hear you were a legend today, in the footy match. Three goals!'

It's an unlikely rescue, but Aaron abandons me to talk football with Alfie, Sid and Carl, and relief floods through me. I sit down on the cliff steps, hugging my knees, trying not to care that I have a boyfriend whose touch makes me shudder. It's not Aaron's fault. He hasn't changed . . . he is exactly the same as always. Confident, good-looking, crazy about football in the same way I am mad about ballet. People say we're a good match, but there is no spark, no energy between us.

I am not sure now if there ever was.

Alfie appears beside me, having abandoned Aaron to Carl and Sid. 'You OK?' he asks, sitting down beside me on the steps. 'You look fed up.'

'Thanks,' I say crossly. 'I'm just . . . tired. I've been practising a lot lately. It's hard work.'

'Ah,' Alfie says. 'The audition. Third Saturday in August, right?'

I blink. 'How do you even know that?'

Alfie looks guilty. 'Um . . . Skye might have mentioned it. Or maybe your mum told my mum, I can't remember. We're all rooting for you, y'know, the whole village. You're going to ace it!'

'It's not that easy,' I sigh.

'I know,' Alfie says. 'Nothing worth having ever is. But you have a talent, Summer, and you're determined . . . you'll do it. Everyone thinks so. Well, almost everyone . . .'

I frown. 'So . . . who thinks I won't?'

Alfie backtracks. 'Nobody,' he says shiftily. 'I mean, we all think you can do it, but I think he just doesn't want to lose you, and that's why he bet you wouldn't get in. I said you would, and we put a tenner on it. My money's safe, I reckon.'

'You had a bet about whether I'd get into ballet school?' I ask, horrified.

'It was just a joke, seriously,' Alfie hedges. 'I was saying you'd pass with flying colours, and he was just arguing for the sake of it. It was nothing personal, Summer. He just doesn't want to accept that you're going away . . .'

I swallow. 'Let me get this straight,' I say. 'You had a bet that I'd get into ballet school, and someone else bet I wouldn't . . .'

'That's about it, yes,' Alfie gulps.

'Let me guess . . . that someone was . . . Aaron?'

Alfie pulls a pained face. 'It's not that he doesn't think you can do it,' he says. 'He just says stuff, to be funny. Different. You know what he's like . . .'

I look towards the firelight, where Aaron is telling Carl and Sid about his third goal of the day and how the team would have been stuffed without him. I can't see a good-looking, popular boy who likes to be funny, just a boy who is self-centred and full of himself, with a mean streak mixed in for good measure. I see somebody I don't like at all.

'Unreal,' I say.

'Me and my big mouth,' Alfie groans. 'I've put my foot in it massively . . . boy, I bet you hate me now.'

'No more than usual,' I sigh, and Alfie puts his head in his hands. 'Look, Alfie, it's not your fault my boyfriend's a creep.'

'He'll kill me,' Alfie whimpers. 'I am dead meat.'

'I won't tell him,' I say. 'Forget it. I guess you didn't tell me anything I didn't already know. It was never going to last.'

Alfie's head springs up again, his eyes wide. 'You're dumping him?' he asks.

'I don't know,' I say. 'I guess . . . we haven't been getting on for a while. No spark.'

'Really?' he asks, his mouth twitching into a smile. 'No spark? It's not all my fault then? Cool. If you ever need to talk . . . about sparks . . . or anything . . . any time . . . I'm here for you, I promise. I mean it, Summer.'

'No thanks,' I say.

'OK. That's cool too,' he shrugs. 'Whatever you like.'

'I'd like you to leave me alone now,' I tell him, and I watch his face fall as he moves off towards the others.

Later, when the sky has darkened to indigo velvet scattered with stars and the bonfire has burnt down to a glow of soft embers, Aaron catches my hand as I dance with Tia, Millie and Cherry on the sand to the sound of Shay's slow guitar.

'Hey,' he says. 'How's my gorgeous girlfriend?'

He pulls me close, and his breath smells of Coke and hamburgers, sweet and greasy at the same time. I turn my face away, up to the stars.

'I've missed you,' he says into my hair, dancing me away across the beach until the bonfire and the music fade into the distance. 'You should have been at the footy match, to support me. You should have been here on the beach this afternoon, and at the party. You're working too hard on this stupid ballet stuff. I called you, but you didn't answer . . .'

'I'm here now,' I whisper, wishing I didn't have to be.

'Yeah. You're here now . . .'

Aaron slides his mouth along my cheek, leaving a trail

of damp like a snail. His hand slithers down to my bum and I wish I was a million miles away, far away from vain, selfish boyfriends who paw you like a piece of meat and make cheap bets that you'll never make your dreams come true.

No spark. Is that a good reason to break up with someone? Tia and Millie might not agree.

Aaron's hands slide over my hip bones. 'Sheesh, Summer,' he says into my ear. 'You eat like a rabbit and lately you're acting like a scared rabbit too. You're getting thin – too thin. There's nothing to hold on to!'

I grab his hands and pull them off me, the way I have wanted to for a long, long time.

'So don't then,' I say. 'Don't bother.'

I turn and run, across the sand, past the bonfire, up the steps and through the midnight garden. People call after me, but I don't listen. I keep on running until I am in my room, and then I throw myself face down on the patchwork quilt Mum made when I was tiny and cry until there are no more tears left.

15

I practise in the senior studio for hours on end, but my movements are heavy, clunky, clumsy, and my head feels fogged with lack of sleep. I lay awake last night crying – I don't even know why. I wish Mum wasn't so far away. She texted earlier to say she was thinking of me. I started tapping out a reply to let her know about Aaron, then deleted it. You can't send a text full of gloom and doom to your mum, not when she's on honeymoon and meant to be enjoying herself.

I bottle up the sadness and practise instead, even though there's no chance today of escaping into the dance. I can't get even the simplest moves right, and Miss Elise pulls me up on it in class.

'Have you had enough sleep, Summer?' she asks, in front

of everyone. 'No more late nights – your dancing isn't up to scratch and you look awful today. You can't afford to party with that audition to work towards! Keep your eye on the prize!'

'Yes, Miss,' I whisper, the criticism twisting inside me like a knife.

If only she knew. The prize is all I think about, but the harder I work the further it seems to slide from my grasp.

I catch the afternoon bus home to Kitnor, get off and find I've walked straight into an ambush. Tia and Millie hook my arms while Skye and Cherry steer me into the Mad Hatter, ordering two strawberry sundaes to share. They want to know what happened last night, of course. I'd kind of like to know myself.

'Is it really over?' Millie asks. 'Forever? For good? Because I thought you were the cutest couple ever! It's so sad!'

'We had nothing to say to each other,' I sigh. 'Nothing in common.'

'You had loads in common,' Tia corrects me. 'You're both popular and clever and good-looking, and both of you have a talent that makes you stand out from the crowd. On paper, you were perfect!'

'In real life, we weren't,' I shrug.

'He does go on a bit about football,' Skye grins. 'And I've always thought his eyes are just a little bit too close together . . .'

I love my sister, I really do.

'There was no spark,' I tell them.

'Well,' Skye says. 'There you are then. You have to have spark.'

Millie just about chokes on her milkshake. 'Spark?' she splutters. 'You're a fine one to talk, Skye Tanberry. There were so many sparks flying between you and Finch last night I thought the two of you would burst into flames any minute!'

Skye blushes and shrugs. 'I like him,' she says simply, and I wonder if it really is that simple. You either like someone or you don't, and at the end of the day I didn't much like Aaron Jones.

'Did you kiss him?' Tia asks my twin. 'Are you going out?'

'Not yet,' Skye laughs. 'Honestly, I've only just met him! And I thought we were talking about Aaron Jones, not Finch!'

'Aaron always seemed so nice,' Millie says wistfully. 'Who

cares about spark? Who cares about whether his eyes are too close together? Not that they are, as far as I can see . . .'

'He bet Alfie Anderson ten pounds I'd fail my ballet school audition,' I reveal, and the girls look shocked. Even Millie throws down her straw in disgust.

'Loser,' Cherry says.

'Idiot,' Skye adds. 'I hated the way he used to paw at you.'

'I hated the way he used to leer at that awful Marisa McKenna,' Tia chips in. 'You're better off without him.'

'Spark,' Millie sighs. 'Maybe you do need it after all.'

The waitress brings our sundaes over and a clutch of long spoons to share. It looks fantastic, but I danced so badly today I know I don't deserve any. I manage to avoid eating more than a single strawberry, and I don't think anyone notices.

'Carl likes you, I'm sure of it, Summer,' Tia muses. 'There are plenty more fish in the sea.'

I shake my head and sip my Coke Zero. Fishing . . . it's just not my thing, and I am tired of feeling out of my depth.

Walking back up the lane towards Tanglewood, Skye and I spot Finch carrying a piece of painted scenery towards

❀ ❀ ❀ ❀ ❀ ❀ ❀ ❀ ❀ ❀ ❀ ❀ ❀ ❀ ❀ ❀ ❀ ❀ ❀

the field by the primary school. Instantly, Skye goes all mushy and starry-eyed, trying to hide under her straw hat.

'Hey, Summer, Skye!' Finch greets us. 'We're turning the school field into an Edwardian fairground for the film. It's awesome – come and see!'

I try to make an excuse, but Skye tugs at my arm, her eyes pleading, and I shrug and follow. The field has been transformed. Workers are setting up swingboats, a helter-skelter, a roundabout with carved carousel horses.

'The funfair's going to be in lots of the shots,' Finch tells us, dropping off his scenery at the gate. 'The film is about the gypsy travellers who worked the fairs at the turn of the last century – this is where they'll shoot most of the crowd scenes this weekend!'

Nobody challenges us as we wander past a hoopla stall, a coconut shy, a Punch and Judy show, a gypsy fortune-telling tent, probably because Finch and Skye are almost part of the crew.

'It's going to be awesome, Summer,' my twin grins. 'Millie and Tia are going to be extras at the weekend, definitely, and Honey and Cherry and Coco. I think you should too . . . it'll help you forget about Aaron.'

'He's forgotten,' I say. 'And no thanks – I have ballet practice.'

'Come on,' Skye says. 'You can take two days out, surely?'

I stare at Skye as if she's on a different planet. Can't she see how much this audition means to me? How hard I'm working? Is she really so preoccupied with Finch? Taking two days out is not an option.

'I can't,' I tell my twin. 'You know that. Dance comes first.'

'Not all the time!' she argues. 'Everyone needs a break sometimes, Summer. I'll be helping with the costumes, I'll find you something cool to wear . . . you'll love it!'

I feel torn. Skye must be worried about me because she wouldn't normally push me this way, but she has it wrong – a weekend playing about on a film set is the last thing I need right now.

'Give it a go,' Finch chips in. 'It'll look good on your CV – shows you can be versatile. You know, something to tell them about at the audition. Dance, film . . . it's all linked, isn't it? Creative?'

I look at Finch, his eyes bright, kind. I try not to dislike him just because my twin is falling in love with him. He is trying to help, and I have to admit he has a point.

'I hadn't thought of it like that . . .'

'Please?' Skye says. 'For me?'

'Oh . . . All right then!'

'*Yesss!*' Skye takes my hands and whirls me round and round, and I can't help it, I am laughing, letting go, perhaps for the first time in weeks. It's August and the sun is shining and a TV film is being made right here in the village – I'd be crazy not to enjoy it.

Finch grabs Skye's straw hat and races away, dodging among the fairground stalls with us following. We stop between the coconut shy and the Hall of Mirrors, catching our breath.

'Wow,' Finch says, stepping towards the shiny distorting mirrors. 'Look at these! Hilarious!'

I look over at his reflection, tall, skinny, with giraffe legs in skinny jeans and a body squashed short with a tiny head. Skye finds a mirror too, one that buckles and turns her body into a swaying, undulating squiggle.

'Freaky!' Finch says. 'I'm like a giant!'

'Look at me!' Skye giggles. 'I'm like a concertina! Weird!'

We are laughing so hard the tears run down our cheeks,

and then I step towards one of the mirrors and the laughter freezes in my throat.

I am not tall, I am not skinny, I am not rippled or wobbly or swaying. My legs are not giraffe-like, my head is not tiny, my face isn't squashed into a frog-eyed whirl or stretched pin-thin. Instead, my reflection fills the whole mirror, like a big, billowing blob. My face is rounder than the moon. My body is square, solid, sickening, my belly is vast, my thighs are thicker than tree trunks and even my ankles look fat.

I know this is a fairground mirror. I know it isn't true, but it feels true, it feels like the real me, exposed at last, huge, hulking, hideous. I am not the girl most likely to succeed, not even close. I am the girl who is fooling everyone, pretending she's OK, working harder and harder to keep the mask in place. When it slips, everyone will see the real me. *You're useless*, the voice in my head reminds me. *A fat, lazy lump*.

No wonder I can't dance, no wonder I'm falling apart inside.

It feels like the end of the world.

16

I am surviving on lettuce leaves and apple slices, and the ache of hunger in my belly has faded to numbness, to nothing. I feel lighter, cleaner, buzzing with energy. I spend my days at the dance school, practising in the senior studio. Hard work always pays off . . . eventually. You just have to keep the faith.

In the evenings, I watch online clips of Sylvie Rochelle in *The Firebird*, looking for inspiration, ideas, while my friends and sisters hang out on the beach or by the gypsy caravans in the woods with Finch and the boys from the film crew.

'Ease up a little,' Skye tells me. 'You're getting obsessed, Summer. It's not healthy.'

But I can't ease up, not if I am going to take two days

out of my schedule to be an extra. I lie awake at night worrying about it, wide awake, my mind racing. Sometimes I get up and creep down to the kitchen to run through my barre exercises again because if you want to be perfect, you can never relax, never stop.

On Sunday morning I am standing in a marquee wearing a straw hat and a white cotton dress with a frilled hem. My long hair is plaited into tight braids, my feet are stuffed into worn leather boots and my face has been painted and powdered and highlighted as if I had a starring role instead of a tiny bit part in a crowd scene.

I agreed to come, but I am regretting it now. Already I've wasted a whole Saturday hanging around doing nothing, and Sunday seems to be going the same way. Skye is busy the whole time, styling and adjusting costumes, but the rest of us have been here for hours, waiting to be called down to the location.

'It'll take your mind off this whole Aaron thing,' Millie says confidently, piling a paper plate with crusty bread and butter and soft French cheese from the buffet table. 'Cheer you up after your heartbreak.'

❀❀❀❀❀❀❀❀❀❀❀❀❀❀❀❀❀❀❀❀❀

'I am not heartbroken, Millie,' I say patiently.

'Of course not,' Tia agrees. 'You're better off without him. Oh, look, there's Carl and Alfie and Finch!'

She drags me over. The three boys are wearing collarless shirts and waistcoats and fusty old breeches that button at the knee, and I have to admit that even if I had been pining for Aaron Jones, this would still have put a smile on my face.

Finch looks quite cool and gypsyish in his tweedy stuff. Carl looks odd but OK, like he has just wandered out of a Victorian family photograph, but Alfie looks just plain deranged. His boots don't fit, his trousers are tattered and he is wearing a floppy brown baker boy hat with his fringe sticking out like a madman. And that's not all.

'Are you wearing eyeliner?' I snort. 'No way!'

Alfie goes a little pink, and I realize with horror that he is also wearing foundation, lip tint and industrial amounts of hair gel.

'It's not my fault,' he complains, backing away into a corner. 'Finch made us come. He said that lots of girls had signed up but not many boys, and that we'd have a laugh. Nobody said anything about make-up! They trowelled it on, seriously!'

'It's not pretty,' I tell him. 'I mean, it is . . . but . . . well, you know what I mean.'

'I will never live this down,' he sighs. 'Anyone could see this film – me, wearing eyeliner and lip tint, in all my hi-definition, widescreen glory. In people's living rooms. What will the lads at school say? I'm not even joking. It cannot be worth it, not for fifty quid.'

'You do have nice eyes, though,' I say, trying not to laugh. 'You could use a little shadow on your lids to bring out the greeny-brown bits . . .'

'Not funny, Summer,' he scowls. 'It's all right for you, you don't mind all this theatrical stuff. I can't stand it. I feel like a prize poodle, trimmed and fluffed and put on show with a bow in its hair.'

'You don't look like a poodle,' I smirk.

'No, I look like a transvestite street urchin,' Alfie groans. 'I can't do this, Summer. I'm serious.'

'Get a grip,' I say sternly. 'You've just got stage fright, Alfie, minus the stage. The minute the cameras start to roll . . .'

Abruptly, Millie steps in front of me, her face pale, eyes wide. 'Don't look over there,' she hisses. 'Take no notice. Don't let it get to you.'

❁❁❁❁❁❁❁❁❁❁❁❁❁❁❁❁❁❁❁❁❁

'Look where?' I ask. 'Don't let what get to me?'

'What are you talking about, Millie?' Alfie demands.

'Nothing!' Millie says, turning me round and herding me away. 'Nothing at all!'

I look back over my shoulder, and that's when I finally notice Aaron. It seems unfair that he should look so handsome in a suit jacket and a faded straw boater when the rest of us are dressed as kids, but that is typical of him. He always comes out on top.

'He wasn't supposed to be here,' Tia tells me, appearing at my other side. 'The boys told him to stay away.'

I expect they did, but Aaron doesn't like being told what to do. The lure of being in a film – and being paid for it – was probably too much for him to resist.

'He shouldn't have come,' Millie huffs. 'Especially not with her!'

I blink, and I wonder just how I could have missed the girl next to Aaron because she certainly stands out from the crowd. Marisa McKenna has crazy, curly dark hair, big gold hoop earrings and a swirly skirt. Unusually for her, it reaches down to her ankles, but her gypsy top dips down carelessly over one golden brown shoulder to reveal a whole lot more cleavage than was usual in Edwardian Britain. Aaron seems transfixed.

I don't blame him, of course. He has just escaped the clutches of a very dull and boring girlfriend, but it didn't take him long to replace me. I do not care about Aaron Jones – I finished with him after all. Marisa McKenna is welcome to him. I wish her well. I hope she doesn't feel too sick when he does his snail-trail kissy thing right down her neck.

I try to speak, try to move, but I seem to be frozen to the spot. Panic churns in my belly and the crush of people begins to blur before my eyes.

'I have to get out of here,' I whisper.

'Summer?' Tia frowns. 'Don't let him see he's upset you. You're letting him win . . .'

'We can't just leave,' Millie says. 'If we miss our calls, we'll miss out on being filmed . . . just ignore him, OK?'

But it's not OK; it's not OK at all.

'She needs fresh air,' Alfie says unexpectedly. 'I'll sort it.'

A ridiculous clown-boy in a floppy baker boy hat puts an arm round me and steers me away, out of the marquee, out across the grass, down to the woods.

17

We sit down beneath the trees, and when I press my face against my knees, a dark, damp patch appears on my skirt.

'Don't,' Alfie says. 'He's not worth it.'

'I know,' I whisper, but I'm not sure I am crying for Aaron Jones at all. I am crying because everything is changing and nothing feels safe any more . . . the life I have planned so carefully and so neatly; my hopes; my dreams; my confidence. It's like picking a hole in an old sweater – before you know it, everything starts to unravel.

Over by the marquee, people are moving. The crew runners are leading crowds of extras down towards the village. Cherry and Honey and their friends are there, and Coco with Humbug on a leash, Carl and Finch and a whole bunch of people from the village, old and young, all dressed up and stepping back in time for a day. My twin sister walks alongside them, tweaking shawls and adjusting hemlines.

I watch Aaron and Marisa stride down across the grass, his arm draped round her shoulder. I spot Millie and Tia, looking around for me. They shout a few times, but I shake my head silently at Alfie and stay hidden beneath the trees.

'We could still go,' Alfie says, handing me a big white hanky. 'Catch them up?'

I wipe my eyes and the hanky comes away stained with pasty beige foundation and streaks of black eyeliner. 'Nah,' I sigh. 'I'm not really in a fairground kind of mood. Do I look a mess?'

'Gorgeous,' Alfie says. 'Almost as pretty as me.'

I laugh, and he blots the hanky against my cheek.

'I didn't want to be in the film anyway,' he shrugs. 'Fame is overrated – I saw that bloke from *Hollyoaks* in the Co-op buying sliced ham yesterday. It took him twenty minutes because he had to sign autographs for a load of kids from the primary school, as well as all the checkout ladies. It's tough at the top.'

'I wouldn't know,' I sigh.

'You will, one day,' Alfie teases. 'You're the "girl most likely to succeed", remember?'

Girl most likely to fall flat on her face more like, a dark voice inside me says ominously. *Useless.* I shake my head, trying to dislodge the words, but they are etched into my mind like barbed wire.

I don't know what is wrong with me lately. I am working harder than I have ever worked before at my ballet, yet still I wake in the middle of the night thinking about the audition, racked by doubts and fears. I have cut out sweet stuff and fatty stuff and junk foods to melt away any last traces of puppy fat, yet when I look in the mirror, I can't see any difference at all. I dump my boyfriend and then freak out the very first time I see him with someone else.

The voice is right. I am useless. I shiver, as if a cloud has passed over the sun.

'Summer?' Alfie says gently. 'Are you OK?'

'I don't know,' I whisper. 'I really don't know any more.'

He doesn't ask stupid questions, which is good because I don't have any answers, not right now. Alfie just puts an arm round me, and it doesn't feel dangerous or predatory, the way it did with Aaron. It feels steady, warm, like someone cares. My eyes drift shut against a sting of tears and my mind stills. After a while, I feel better, calmer, stronger. The voice in my head is silent now and the churning in my stomach has faded.

I open my eyes. Alfie Anderson has his arm round me casually, easily, like it is no big deal. He is not cracking jokes at my expense or trying to wind me up, just frowning slightly as he gazes off into the distance. This is deeply weird.

'You're not over him, are you?' he asks quietly, and I blink.

'Aaron?' I say. 'Trust me, I am totally, one hundred per cent over him. I ditched him, remember? Things weren't working out – no spark.'

'Oh yeah,' Alfie echoes. 'No spark.'

He cracks a smile and faint patches of pink appear in his cheeks . . . or maybe he let the make-up girl dust him with blusher too; it's hard to be sure with Alfie.

'I am not pining for Aaron,' I promise. 'I just got a shock, I suppose. I didn't expect to see him here, especially not with Marisa.'

'He must be mad,' Alfie says. 'You're a million times prettier than Marisa. And you're clever and talented and popular too . . . you're amazing, Summer Tanberry, you know that, right?'

There's a silence, a long, empty silence. I think Alfie Anderson just paid me a compliment, and a pretty big one too. He's just trying to make me feel better, I know. This is Alfie Anderson after all. He does not have a romantic bone in his body.

'Watch out,' I say, jabbing him gently in the ribs as I get to my feet, brushing the twigs and fallen leaves from my clothes. 'I knew you couldn't stay away from the wind-ups for long. You're good, Alfie, I'll give you that. Anyone would think you were serious!'

'As if,' Alfie says, a little sadly.

'I'm not going to bother with boys from now on,' I declare, crunching my way out of the woods towards the rickety stile. 'I have to focus on ballet. I wish I hadn't let them talk me into this. I've missed practice, and now I'll have to work all afternoon to make up for it. I have to be perfect for the audition . . .'

I clamber over the stile, but as I swing down into the field, my head swims and the world shifts and suddenly I am seeing stars.

'Hey,' Alfie is saying. 'Whoa, Summer . . . what's up?'

He takes my hand, steadies me, and the world shifts back again. I take a deep breath and my head clears and the stars fade.

'I just felt a bit faint for a minute there,' I whisper.

'When did you last eat?' Alfie asks. 'Eat properly, I mean?'

I sigh. 'I had an apple for breakfast. Fruit is good for you.'

'Breakfast was hours ago,' he tells me. 'And fruit is great, but you can't keep going all day on one poxy apple. You'll make yourself ill.'

Anger bubbles up inside me, and I push it firmly down again.

'I don't want to talk about it,' I say. 'You don't get it, Alfie, OK? It's tough being a dancer – really tough. It's not just about talent, you have to look right.'

'You haven't been eating properly since before school broke up,' Alfie argues.

'Back off, Alfie,' I insist. 'I'm eating plenty . . . I just skipped lunch because of the whole filming thing. Their buffet table was all potato salad and French bread and full-fat cheese . . .'

'Bread and cheese and potatoes aren't bad for you,' he says.

127

'I know, but . . . look, it's only for a little while . . .'

'Are you sure?' His brown eyes search mine, and I have to look away.

We walk down across the grass towards the marquee, still holding hands, and I am glad that my sisters and my friends are not here to see us because, boy, would they have a field day with that. They would not understand that we are only holding hands because of the way I felt woozy a few minutes earlier.

I hope Alfie understands that, come to think of it.

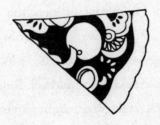

18

I head to the dance studio – maybe there I'll remember who I'm meant to be. After losing my cool earlier with Aaron and making an idiot of myself with Alfie, I am not sure I recognize myself. I am not the kind of person who loses the plot in public, who runs away from an ex-boyfriend and ends up sharing my secret fears with the most annoying boy in school . . . except that now I am.

Dancing might not be going as well as I'd like it to, but it helps, all the same. My body feels stretched and worked and the guilt of missing yesterday's practice is a little less sharp, the memories of this afternoon's embarrassment less shameful. I am still no further forward with my set piece, though. I have two weeks to come up with something creative and dramatic, something that will wow Sylvie Rochelle, yet I cannot seem to dredge up even the tiniest spark of originality.

Then, coming out of a pirouette spin, the room tilts suddenly and I lose my footing and fall. For a second or two I lie still, crumpled on the floor, my head whirling, the music swooping on in the background; then the fog lifts and I sit up, a little shakily.

I switch off the CD and pad softly through to the changing rooms. My left side is a little sore and bruised, but my pride has taken the biggest knock. At least nobody was around to see my fall this time, but two faints in one day? That can't be coincidence. Could Alfie be right about the skipping meals and eating properly thing? I frown. Suppose I fainted and fell in an actual dance lesson? Or, worse still, during my audition? I can't risk that, no way.

I get changed quickly. I want to get away, out of the dance school, away from the studio, but I can't go home yet. I don't want to face my sisters, or their questions. I head for the library and sit for a while in the quiet, using the computer to google dance audition tips. Be prepared, the websites suggest. Practise hard. There are no tips for producing an expressive dance out of thin air . . . I guess that would be asking too much. I google 'Firebird', and watch online clips of slim, beautiful ballerinas pushing themselves to the limit. If they can do it, why can't I?

Because you're weak, the voice in my head says smugly. *Weak and lazy and greedy.*

I wince. I don't want to be any of those things, of course, but I don't want to faint in class either . . . maybe there are smarter ways to cut back on calories. I check out a couple of books on diet and healthy eating, promising myself I'll read up on nutrition, then catch the late bus home. As it chugs along, I check my mobile, expecting texts from Skye, Tia and Millie asking if I'm OK. Nothing. Did they miss me at all? Or maybe they're still filming? I try not to mind.

There is one from Mum at least – telling me that she and Paddy are now in Cuzco, getting used to the higher altitudes before trekking up to Machu Picchu. I want to call her right now and ask her to jump on a plane and come home because I need her, need to talk, need a hug. I don't, of course. Instead, I tap out a chirpy message telling her I'm fine, that practice is going well. It wouldn't do to let the mask slip, would it?

When I get home, my sisters – and Finch – are loafing

on the squashy blue sofas, eating takeaway pizzas and endlessly rerunning the day. They can't shut up about the fairground scene and the filming, the costumes and the candyfloss, the thrill of it all.

'You're back!' Skye says as I come in. 'Honestly, Summer, you should have stayed – you missed the most amazing day!'

'Tia and Millie said you changed your mind,' Finch says. 'Got bored and decided to practise instead . . .'

That's why Skye didn't text then. I suppose I should be grateful that Tia and Millie covered for me.

'It's important,' I say, squeezing on to the end of one sofa. 'This audition . . .'

Honey rolls her eyes and Coco throws a cushion at me and says that I never talk about anything except the audition any more, and it's beyond boring.

I feel as though I've been slapped, but Coco doesn't mean to hurt me, I know. Is that really what my sisters think? That ballet is boring? That my dream is dull, pointless, pitiful? Spots of colour burn in my cheeks. I feel a million miles away from my sisters right now, an alien creature, outside looking in.

They don't even notice I'm upset. You'd think the lot of

them are heading for Hollywood any minute, the way they are talking. Skye wants to be a costume designer, Cherry a scriptwriter; Honey wants to be a movie star and Coco wants to train animals for films because she met a woman who did just that for a living. Finch has been asked to play a bit part in the rest of the film, as one of the gypsies. It's a non-speaking part, but still, he is dreaming of fame and fortune.

'They said I had something,' he muses. 'A kind of spark!'

'You do,' Skye tells him, wide-eyed. 'Definitely. You were awesome. Me, I've never worked so hard, only it didn't feel like work, not one bit. Best day of my life, I swear!'

She lines up a DVD of *Breakfast at Tiffany's*, Grandma Kate's favourite film. I like it too because it stars Audrey Hepburn who was very beautiful and very thin and once trained to be a ballet dancer.

Finch leans down to read the DVD box. He's squished so close to Skye you'd think they were joined at the hip. It feels odd to see my twin with a boy. A few weeks ago I was the one with a boyfriend; things have turned upside down, and I am not sure I like it. It's impossible not to like Finch, but it feels like he is all Skye is thinking about right now.

Grandma Kate comes in and everyone settles down as

133

the DVD begins. We watch the waiflike Audrey Hepburn sitting on a window ledge singing 'Moon River', the saddest, most beautiful song in the world, as the last of the pizza is handed round. I let it go by me.

Skye looks up briefly, her brows slanted into a frown. 'Not hungry?' she asks. 'You love pizza, Summer!'

'I ate at the dance school,' I lie. 'You know me, I always have an appetite after practice . . .'

Skye looks at me for a long moment, thoughtful, but then Finch nudges her and I am forgotten. My heart thumps. I am not sure whether to be relieved or disappointed. Mum's not here, but maybe I could talk to Skye about all this?

Or maybe not. Skye is the person who knows me best in the world, but she has no idea I'm struggling. I am right here, in the middle of my family, yet I have never felt more alone. What's happening to me? Why can't somebody see what's wrong? Skye is miles away, in some kind of fantasy world with Finch, their hands entwined as they watch the screen. I look at Grandma Kate and wish she wasn't quite so easy to fool, or that Mum didn't have to be on the other side of the world.

19

On Thursday Miss Elise asks us to show her our expressive dance pieces, and I panic. I seem to have lost the ability to turn music into dance. The sequences I've put together so far feel forced, awkward – they don't hang together properly, and I feel like I am wearing clumpy boots instead of pointe shoes.

Miss Elise shakes her head. 'Summer, that's not good enough,' she says quietly. 'What's going on? It's a strong piece of music, but the dance doesn't match up to it. It's rough, unformed, amateurish. Haven't you been working on it?'

My face floods scarlet. 'I have, of course,' I whisper.

'Then work harder!' Miss Elise says. 'This is one thing I can't help you with – it has to be your creativity, your interpretation of the music. The piece you've chosen is all about passion, fire . . . but I'm not getting any of that from your choreography. Your expressive dance has to be perfect for the audition, Summer; you don't need me to tell you that!'

No, I don't . . . I tell myself exactly the same thing every other minute. I fight back tears. 'Sorry, Miss Elise.'

She claps her hands to dismiss Jodie and Sushila, and they shoot me sympathetic glances as they go through to get changed.

My teacher sighs. 'You're one of the best pupils I have had here for a very long time,' she says briskly. 'You have potential – good technical skills and a spirited, expressive style that sets you apart. Those are the reasons Sylvie Rochelle picked you out . . . so where are those qualities now? These last two weeks you've been tired, slow, lack-lustre. You've always struck me as one of the most dedicated, determined students I have, yet you seem to have just stopped trying!'

'No!' I protest. 'That's not true!'

'Do you realize what a fantastic opportunity this is?' she asks. I nod, mute.

'Then show me, Summer,' she says, exasperated. 'The auditions are two weeks away. Be ready. Don't let me down. This won't happen all by itself – you have to work at it, you have to be serious about it.'

'I am serious!'

'Push yourself,' Miss Elise says. 'Find the spark, the passion. You can do it, I know you can!'

Spark again. That elusive quality I just don't have – not with boys, not with dancing, maybe not at all. When did I lose it? Can I find it again, set it alight with the fire of my determination? Miss Elise's words cut deep, but I smile, even though I feel like crying.

Later Jodie and I sit in the cafe down by the seafront, sipping skinny lattes. 'Miss Elise was totally picking on you today,' Jodie says. 'She can be a real slave-driver sometimes. You danced fine, Summer. Not your best maybe, but everyone has an off day sometimes. You should have told her, you know.'

'Told her what?' I frown.

'About breaking up with Aaron,' Jodie says. 'You said in the changing rooms it was no big deal, but it's got to have put you off your stride, seeing him with that horrible girl and everything.'

'It was nothing to do with Aaron,' I say.

'Your mum and stepdad are away,' Jodie continues, 'and you've got all those film people staying in the house. That'll be stressful too. You should have explained!'

'I'm fine,' I say, stirring my latte. 'It's nothing to do with any of that. I don't get it, Jodie – she thinks I'm not serious, not trying. I mean, is she kidding? I practise every single day, for hours! It's all I ever think about lately!'

Jodie licks the strawberry jam off her scone thoughtfully. 'Maybe you're trying too hard,' she considers. 'Overdoing it. I practise every day too, but not for hours and hours. It'd drive me nuts. Maybe you're doing too much? Getting – I don't know, stale? You are looking a bit tired, you know.'

I sigh. 'Miss Elise thinks I'm not serious enough. You think I'm working too hard. I can't win, can I?'

Jodie shrugs, spooning up a curl of clotted cream. 'You just seem a bit stressed, that's all,' she says. 'It's such a big thing, isn't it? But it's all down to fate in the end, you know. If it's meant to happen, it will. If not . . . well, we have to accept it.'

This is not what I want to hear. Fate is way too fickle – I

❀❀❀❀❀❀❀❀❀❀❀❀❀❀❀❀❀❀❀❀❀

can't step back and allow it to steer my life. Taking control is the only way.

'Do your best,' Jodie is saying. 'Obviously. But don't let it take over your life!'

It's a bit too late for that, of course. This dream has been driving my life ever since I can remember, and I have never been closer to touching it. Now is not the time to relax the pressure. Just over a fortnight from now, the auditions will be done and dusted, but until then I cannot, will not stop trying.

'I just want to get a place,' I say. 'I have to make them think I'm right for that course. I'm doing everything I can think of!'

'Me too,' Jodie says, biting into her cream scone. 'Don't get me wrong – I'd do anything.'

Anything but cut back on calories, obviously.

I must be staring because Jodie raises an eyebrow. 'Want a bit?' she asks, holding out her plate with the other half of the scone. 'I thought you were being a bit strict, just having a skinny latte. This is gorgeous! Home-made, I think!'

'Do – do you ever worry about your weight?' I ask clumsily. 'Your shape?'

A slow flush seeps over Jodie's cheeks, and I wish I could bite my tongue. Of course Jodie worries – she's human after all, but I know that she is pretty confident and happy with her body these days. I just wish I could say the same.

'I think I'm OK as I am,' she says a little stiffly. 'Dancing keeps me slim, and I like having some curves. What are you trying to say?'

'Nothing!' I protest. 'I think you're fine too, Jodie. But . . . I'm not sure that I am. I thought that if I could be slimmer, lighter, I might stand more chance at the auditions. And I am trying to cut back. No more cake, no more junk food . . . but it's so hard!'

Jodie blinks. 'You're cutting back?' she echoes. 'Dieting? But there's nothing of you to start with!'

'That's not true!' I argue. 'I used to be slim, but these days I'm huge. Maybe it's puppy fat, but I look like a Labrador in a leotard. It's gross.'

Jodie looks horrified. 'Er, no, Summer,' she says. 'There's no way you look big – you're not built that way. And you don't have puppy fat, not a scrap – you're more whippet than Labrador, trust me. You have lost some weight lately – I thought you were just working too hard. You have to eat. Please don't lose any more!'

I look at Jodie. Does she actually want me to be fat? Probably because that way she won't look so bad herself. I flinch at the thought, but why else would Jodie be so negative? Is she jealous?

'We all get a bit more rounded as we grow up, you know,' she is saying. 'That's normal. You can't diet that away!'

I can, I think stubbornly. I will.

'What else have you been cutting out?' she asks. 'It's not just cake, is it? You're dieting properly, I know you are, and that's a really, really bad idea. We're thirteen, Summer – that's way too young for crash diets. Now, of all times, you need to be strong! You need your vitamins and minerals and protein, or you won't be able to dance your best!'

'I'm not stupid, Jodie!' I snap. 'D'you think I'd take risks with something so important? It's not a diet, honestly. I've just ditched the junk food . . .'

I frown. This might have been true a couple of weeks ago, but things have gone way past that point now. I am skipping meals, making excuses, feeding my dinner to Fred the dog when nobody is looking, and fainting. Deep down, I know that isn't right.

I don't think Jodie is fooled either. My eyes blur with tears, and she slides into the booth beside me, puts her arms round me. Words leak out and I cannot seem to stop them.

'I can't help it,' I whisper. 'I have to pass this audition, I have to! I can't give them any excuse to turn me down!'

'But you're not eating enough,' Jodie says softly. 'That's why your dance isn't working, why you're tired and slow in class. You're hungry and weak and worn out.'

I drag a hand across my eyes, furious, swallowing back the tears. 'I'm fine,' I say crossly. 'I wish I hadn't said anything. I thought you'd understand!'

'I do understand,' she says. 'You're all stressed out over this audition. I know how much you want it – I feel exactly the same – but you can't let it take over. You have to eat!'

'It's only for a few weeks,' I whisper. 'Don't tell anyone, Jodie, please!'

'I won't,' she promises. 'But . . . Summer, you have to see. Food isn't your enemy, it's fuel. If you starve yourself, you'll get ill and then you won't be able to dance at all! I'm getting you something to eat, OK?'

I stare at the tabletop. I must look a mess, a frantic girl with a pink, tear-stained face, falling to pieces in public. I am normally so cool, so polite, so together . . . but this is the second time in a week I have lost the plot. What's happening to me?

'Listen to me, Summer,' Jodie is saying. 'It'll be OK. You just need to eat. I'll get you something, and then you'll feel better, OK?'

As if it could ever be that easy. 'OK. I'll try.'

Jodie goes up to the counter. She is trying to help, I know – isn't she? I can't tell any more. What if there's only room for one of us at Rochelle Academy? If Jodie sees me as a threat and wants to sabotage my chances?

My head aches with thinking about it all. Jodie isn't like that, I know. She's not mean or spiteful or competitive. She's just worried, and she might have a point because the truth is I didn't dance well today and I feel so tired, so muddled. Then Jodie sets a tray down on the table, grinning, and it all becomes clear.

Don't even think about it, the voice in my head warns. As if.

A tall glass of strawberry milkshake, topped with fresh fruit and an ice-cream float, a vast slice of chocolate sponge

cake, oozing cream and jam and topped with thick chocolate buttercream . . . I could put on weight just looking
at it.

Is she serious? I look at Jodie's stupid grin and wonder
why I ever thought she was my friend. I grab my ballet bag
and slam out of the cafe, and I don't look back.

20

Jodie's betrayal is like a knife twisting inside me. She doesn't want me to be slim; she's jealous because I have the self-control to say no to cake and junk food. Alfie has noticed my eating too, and he doesn't understand either. How long before Miss Elise notices, before Grandma Kate and my sisters start to ask questions?

They'll all try to stop me, if I let them. That can't happen.

It's Saturday, and I'm helping Skye with the room-changes – Cherry is out with Shay and Coco is helping Harry in the chocolate workshop. Honey, surprise, surprise, is still in bed. She was out last night with JJ, and I am pretty sure she came home later than the eleven o'clock curfew too. Grandma Kate didn't seem to notice, but I did.

I treat the room-changes as a kind of exercise, stripping

the beds and making them up with fresh sheets and duvet covers, dusting, hoovering, scrubbing the bathrooms. I was tired yesterday from dance practice, but still, I couldn't sleep; dark thoughts kept racing through my mind, doubts, fears, worries. Today I'm so weary I could curl up and sleep on the newly made beds.

'OK?' Skye asks, popping her head round the door. 'Finished?'

'Just about.' For a minute I think about talking to my twin, telling her about the knot of fear that has lodged itself in my belly these last few weeks. But what would I say? That I can't sleep, can't eat, can't think straight? That I am chasing a dream, yet afraid to catch it? None of it makes sense.

Skye hasn't a clue how I am feeling. I promised myself I'd work on staying close to my twin this summer, but right now we are miles apart. Skye has other things on her mind. She used to know what I was thinking even before I did, but lately, I have fallen right off her radar. I don't think she'd notice if I fell down dead right in front of her, she is so wrapped up with Finch.

'I'm going down to the crew field to help Jess with the costumes,' she says. 'They're using Finch in quite a few of the main scenes now. Cool, huh? He looks great in all that vintage stuff! See you later!'

'See you, Skye.'

Grandma Kate has gone to the village to shop, so I take my library books down to the hammock to read. I have to find out how to eat and still lose weight, how to make sure nobody worries or tries to interfere. When you don't eat, people start to notice – and they don't like it.

I will just have to be more careful.

The books explain it all . . . which foods are low in calories but high in protein, to help you stay healthy while losing weight. I make a list. Tuna, cold chicken, boiled eggs, cottage cheese, low-fat yoghurt. Salad leaves, tomatoes, sweetcorn, celery. Today I have eaten a boiled egg and an apple, which seems fairly OK.

Of course the books also tell you to eat bread and potatoes and pasta and rice; cheese and lamb and pork and quiche and pastry and pie; they say that it's OK to have a slice of pizza or a Chinese takeaway once in a while, or even a square or two of chocolate, a pudding, a cookie, a cake.

I know better. Those foods aren't for dancers.

I like making those things, though, and perhaps if

Grandma Kate sees me cooking and baking, she won't notice I am not actually eating the end results. It'll take willpower, of course, but I have plenty of that.

I watch from the hammock as Harry comes out of the workshop in a chocolate-streaked apron to greet the postman, collecting a handful of orders for Paddy's luxury truffles. Even my new stepdad peddles high-class junk food, fat and sugar parcelled up in pretty boxes. No wonder I'm fat. It's a miracle the whole family aren't the size of hippos.

I list down meal ideas to make for my sisters: pizza, pasta, nachos, quiche . . . apple tart, trifle, tiramisu. My mouth waters just thinking about them. Next I list practice times and lesson times and times to swim and chill out with my sisters and my friends too. I will not let Aaron Jones or anyone else accuse me of being obsessed or boring, of having a one-track mind. I will not let him tell me that I need to get a life. I will show everyone, myself included, that I can do it all. I will toughen up, learn to hide my fears – I will not lose it in front of my friends, let them see me upset.

'You're the sensible, organized one,' Tia has always told me. 'You've got everything under control.'

❀❀❀❀❀❀❀❀❀❀❀❀❀❀❀❀❀❀❀❀

Yeah, right. The trouble is that when your friends and family are used to seeing you succeed, they don't always notice when you start to fail. Maybe they just don't want to see. Well, fine. I may not have been much use as an extra in the film, but I have pretty good acting skills all the same. I show people what they want to see, hide the stuff they'd rather not know about. So what if the mask has slipped a couple of times?

I will just have to try harder at keeping it in place.

I wake up to the sound of Fred barking. The sun is high, my library books have slipped on to the grass and Humbug the lamb is chomping her way through Mum's herb garden.

I stretch and yawn and peer over the side of the hammock, and there is Alfie Anderson walking across the garden towards me. I gather up the books in a panic, stuffing them under the hammock cushions and leaning back on them to make sure they stay hidden.

'Skye's not here,' I say, as he approaches.

'I know,' he grins. 'I came to see you.'

I struggle to sit up. 'I'm fine,' I tell him brightly. 'Thanks for looking out for me the other day . . . I think I had a bit of a bug. That's why I hadn't eaten, why I felt woozy for a little while. It was kind of you to sit with me.'

Alfie flops down on the grass beside the hammock, his face unreadable. I'm not sure the lie has fooled him.

'It wasn't kind of me,' he shrugs. 'I wanted to. I'm glad you're feeling better. How's the dance practice going?'

'Great,' I say, with a little more enthusiasm than necessary. 'Really good.'

'How many days till the audition?'

'Twelve days, twenty-one hours and fifteen minutes,' I grin. 'Not that I'm counting.'

Alfie nods. He looks thoughtful, sitting under the trees in the dappled sunlight, his floppy mid-brown hair freshly washed after its midweek gel-fest, face scrubbed clean of everything but freckles. I suppose I am not the only one growing up – Alfie has shaken off the scruffy, slightly deranged look I have always associated with him. He is tall and stylish these days in band T-shirts and rolled-up jeans, his grin wide and easy.

'No eyeliner today?' I quip.

'I'm trying out the natural look.'

About a lifetime goes by, or possibly just a minute or two, with me swaying in the hammock and Alfie sprawled across the grass. I think about telling him I am busy, that he should go, that I have a dance class in town or have promised to help in the chocolate workshop, but the words won't come.

I pick a daisy from the grass, pierce the stalk with my thumbnail and thread another one through. I loved making daisy chains when I was little. I'd make bracelets and necklaces and daisy earrings . . . I loved the way each tiny flower was perfect on its own but better still linked together. It was the way I felt about Mum and Dad, about Skye and Honey and Coco, all the people I loved.

'Hey,' Dad said once, one warm day when I'd made a crown of daisies for my hair. 'My little princess.'

I really felt like a princess that day. That was before Dad left, of course. I may have been Dad's little princess, but it didn't stop him breaking the family up. Daisy chains are pretty fragile, and it turns out that families are too. Sometimes we love people who just don't love us back – or at least not enough.

'I can't do it,' Alfie says, watching me make a circle of daisies. 'Too clumsy. I'm all fingers and thumbs.'

I hang my circle of daisies from Alfie's ear. 'It would have looked better with eyeliner,' I say. 'But still, not a bad look.'

Alfie laughs. 'You just don't take me seriously, do you? Still, anything that takes your mind off the audition has to be good . . .'

'Nothing can,' I shrug.

'It's your dream, I suppose,' Alfie says quietly. 'Dancing.'

'Totally. Major dream. Always has been . . .'

'I'm not sure I have dreams like that,' he says. 'I used to want to be Superman, when I was a kid. Then I thought I might be a stand-up comic, have my own show on the TV and all that. Not sure about that either any more. I'm fed up of acting the clown.'

'You get trapped,' I say. 'People start to see you a certain way. They get so used to it that they stop actually looking, even if you're not that way any more.'

Just like I dismissed Alfie years ago as the most annoying boy in the western hemisphere, and never bothered to check that the label still fitted. It doesn't seem to, not any more. I wonder what people see when they look at me. Little Miss Perfect, Tia once called me when we'd fallen out briefly over a team project at school. At the time, I'd been torn between hurt that she was angry and pride that the word 'perfect' could be applied to me, even as an insult.

Is that what they think? That it all comes easily?

'I'm considering alternative careers,' Alfie says. 'I was thinking maybe a TV chef, but after the eyeliner experience, I'm not sure I'm cut out for the cameras. Maybe I'll just run a very cool organic restaurant or something.'

'Are you kidding?' I ask.

He holds his hands up. 'Deadly serious,' he says. 'In fact, I made something I thought you might like . . . just a little sweet treat . . .'

No, no, no, roars the voice in my head.

'Alfie,' I say carefully, through gritted teeth. 'You were kind to me the other day, but really, I promise, I'm fine. I don't need you or anyone else to look out for me.'

Alfie shrugs. 'OK,' he says. 'I can't stay anyhow . . . but I may as well leave this. No worries if you don't like it. It was just a thought.'

He takes a small Tupperware box out of his rucksack and hands it to me, getting to his feet. 'See you around, Summer.'

He walks away and I fight the impulse to throw the box at the back of his head. Just when I was starting to see him

153

as a friend, I can see that he is no friend at all – he's just like Jodie, a busybody trying to sabotage my eating.

I rip the lid off the box, expecting to see chocolate cake, trifle, sticky toffee pudding. Instead, I see chunks of pineapple, halved strawberries and dark red raspberries sprinkled with fresh mint. My mouth waters, and I start to smile.

21

I force myself to start eating three small meals a day, fruit for breakfast and tuna or chicken or cottage cheese salad for lunch and tea. It's worth it if it keeps people off my case, and the fancy dinners I am preparing to help Grandma Kate out are a pretty good distraction too. Nobody seems to notice that I'm not eating anything much myself, or that Fred the dog is getting podgy on all the extras I feed him under the table.

The dizzy spells stop, so I push myself harder. I plough my energy into my dancing, and find that the fog has lifted and I can move freely again, spin and leap and pirouette. The fear of failure begins to retreat slightly.

I try yet again to choreograph my expressive dance. I think myself into the mind of one of the enchanted creatures bewitched by the firebird, dancing madly to their destruction, and this time, finally, the sequences flow. Miss Elise says the dance is starting to come together, and relief floods through me. If I practise, work really, really hard, I might still manage to do this. I cross the days off the calendar: twelve, eleven, ten.

Mum texts from Peru to say that she and Paddy have left Cuzco and are trekking up to Machu Picchu. **Hard work,** she says. **But amazing views. How is the practice going? Everything OK?**

What can I say? I wouldn't even know where to start.

All well, I text back. **Don't worry – everything is under control.**

Well, almost.

Honey has discovered that her geek-guy mate, Anthony, is home alone for the whole weekend while his parents visit an aged relative in Wales. She swings into action, planning a party.

'He lives out on the edge of the village,' she says, ransacking the freezer for burgers and frozen bread rolls. 'No neighbours . . . we can really let loose!'

❀❀❀❀❀❀❀❀❀❀❀❀❀❀❀❀❀❀❀❀❀

'Does Anthony actually know?' I ask, as my big sister sneaks a bottle of fizzy wine out from the rack and drops it into her bag.

'He suggested it,' she shrugs. 'At least he said I should come over for a barbie, and that's just about the same thing . . .'

I raise an eyebrow. Anthony came to my birthday party in February and trailed around after Honey while she flirted with every boy in the place. She threw him just enough smiles to keep him sweet, and I am guessing she will twist him round her little finger this time too.

'Come on, Summer,' Honey says. 'His idea of a good social life is playing non-stop online war games with other random geek-boys. He needs a bit of real-life fun for a change. I've asked everyone. Apart from Aaron – I told him not to show his ugly face!'

'Thanks,' I sigh. 'But are you sure you want us there, Honey? You never used to invite us places.'

'It's different now,' Honey shrugs. 'You're more grown-up. Besides, if we all go, Grandma Kate won't start thinking I'm up to something!'

'Are you up to something?'

Honey's eyes widen. 'Of course not!'

❀❀❀❀❀❀❀❀❀❀❀❀❀❀❀❀❀❀

Anthony's party is in full swing. The garden is stuffed with people – someone has opened a window and set up speakers on the sill and the *thud-thud-thud* of R & B booms out above the smell of charred meat and smoke.

I should be practising, I know, but my friends and sisters have dragged me along and now, to top it all, Alfie appears at my elbow.

'You again,' I sigh.

'Me again,' he grins. 'How's the practice going? Not long now, right?'

'A week tomorrow it'll all be over,' I say.

Anthony ushers us over towards the barbeque where JJ and Honey are cooking sausages, burgers and sweetcorn cobs cocooned in foil. 'Enjoy yourselves,' he gushes. 'Honey's awesome – she organized all this! I didn't know how many friends I really had until now!'

I am not sure that the kids crowded round the barbie are Anthony's friends, though. They don't seem to notice him at all.

Honey waves and hands me a burger loaded with salad and relish and melting cheese, wrapped in a soft, white roll. 'Ditch the diet, little sister,' she whispers. 'Live a little.'

I flinch at her words. So even Honey has noticed I am eating less? That's worrying. I abandon the burger on a nearby picnic table when nobody is looking.

'It goes to show,' Anthony is saying, looking round the garden. 'You don't have to be one of the cool kids to have friends. Who'd have thought that someone like your sister would want to be mates with me? OK, I'm just helping her with schoolwork, but still, people sit up and take notice. Some of the lads used to pick on me, but now I'm friends with Honey, all that has stopped. Look at me now!'

I look at Anthony, a small, stocky boy with pasty skin and glinting eyes that look a little too intense behind thick horn-rimmed glasses. His gaze drifts over to Honey with that same puppy-dog loyalty I noticed back in February. She has him dangling on a string like a human yo-yo. One minute she is reeling him in with a winning smile and a flutter of her lashes; the next minute she lets him go again and he crashes to the floor.

'Well, you're very welcome to come along to ours some

time,' I say politely. 'We have beach parties now and then. You'd like it.'

'Thanks!' he says, puppy-dog keen.

'Any more punch, Anthony?' Honey calls, and while he bounds off to fetch her a drink, my big sister pulls JJ close for a big smoochy kiss.

'Is she going out with JJ?' Alfie asks. 'Only Anthony's pretty smitten, isn't he? And I thought she fancied Marty from the crew field. They were pretty flirty at the beach party the other weekend . . .'

'That's Honey,' I shrug. 'She's kind of hard to pin down.'

There's a whoop of laughter from the doorway as Chris, Marty and a bunch of younger people from the crew field spill out across the grass, drinks in hand. Honey pulls them into her circle, and they clump round her like planets orbiting the sun.

I spot Finch with his arm round Skye's shoulder, whispering into her hair. I wave them over, but they just smile, their eyes sliding away from me. Nobody much exists for them right now except each other, and dark resentment bubbles inside me. I am happy for Skye, and I like Finch, but I can't help thinking he's taking my twin away from me, just when I need her most.

On my other side, Shay and Cherry are laughing and Millie and Tia are chatting up a couple of high school boys. I try to join in with the chat, but they are talking about last weekend's filming, days at the beach I haven't shared, shopping trips to town I've missed out on. Ballet practice has eaten up my days lately, my life, left me stranded on the edge of things with nothing to say.

I watch my little sister Coco with her friends, looking very grown-up for just-turned twelve. I am so used to Coco looking small and young for her age that it's a shock to notice that she's not a little girl any more. She's wearing lipgloss and sparkly eyeshadow, and blushes furiously every time a good-looking boy walks past. I must be some kind of freak because I don't think I want anything to do with boys, not ever again.

It's as if growing up is a sickness, spreading faster and faster like a flu bug in winter, turning everything upside down. Right now, I feel immune to it, an outsider looking in, slightly horrified at the chaos it can cause. Sometimes I think I'd like to freeze myself in time, or pedal backwards a little to when I was nine or ten and things weren't quite so complicated.

'Is that a trampoline down at the bottom of the garden?' Alfie asks brightly, tugging me back to reality. 'Didn't have you down as a gymnast, Anthony?'

'It's my sister's,' he shrugs. 'She never uses it any more. She grew out of it.'

'Cool,' says Alfie. 'Like I grew out of practical jokes and jelly and ice cream and pedal cars.'

But I can't help thinking it's not cool at all that we have to grow out of the things we love.

22

I slip away from the crowded patio and down through the apple trees, through the cool grass to the trampoline. I look at it and smile, thinking of long ago times in Tia's garden, laughing, jumping, reaching for the sky.

I clamber up and get my balance, bouncing experimentally. Then I am jumping, big joyful leaps, stretching and curling, making my own rhythm, letting the trampoline take me higher and higher. The jumping becomes a dance, a meditation, as natural as breathing.

The light around me fades and darkens, and someone changes the R & B soundtrack for something indie. Through the apple trees I can see tea-light lanterns glinting. If I tilt back my head and stretch my arms up high, I could almost snatch a star out of the sky.

❀❀❀❀❀❀❀❀❀❀❀❀❀❀❀❀❀❀❀

'Room for one more?' a voice asks, and Alfie Anderson hauls himself up beside me. He starts to jump and straight away the rhythm changes, throwing me off balance. Alfie crashes into me, howling, and I push him to arm's length, laughing in spite of myself. This is how it used to be in Tia's garden when we were little – me and Skye and Tia and Millie all jumping together, a mess of bodies colliding and crashing into each other, screams of laughter, fun.

'Alfie!' I screech. 'Watch what you're doing!'

'Can't!' he yelps. 'Can't even see! This is crazy!'

His hand latches on to mine in the dark and finally we are jumping in time, mouths stretched wide with laughter, my long hair snaking out to brush his face as we jump. And then the rhythm collapses into chaos and we stagger and yell and fall down in a heap, breathless. I try to scramble up, but Alfie pulls me down.

'Leave it, Summer,' he says. 'Let go. You've been exercising for ages . . . you must be tired.'

Never enough, the voice in my head insists. *Lazy, lazy, lazy. Push harder!*

I try again to get up, but Alfie holds on tightly to my hand.

'It's OK, Summer,' he says. 'Really. It's OK.'

And part of me believes him, so I stop struggling and lie back, catching my breath, feeling the ache of tiredness in my muscles, the springy stretch of the trampoline beneath my back. My fingers seem to burn where they are touching Alfie's. I sit up abruptly, breaking away, moving to the edge of the trampoline so I can let my legs dangle. Alfie crawls over to join me.

'That was fun,' he says, still breathless.

'Yeah.' I rake a hand through my hair and rescue the flower clip which has slipped down behind one ear, fixing it back in place.

'I like the flower,' Alfie says.

'I like the flower too,' I echo. 'Aaron gave it to me, before we were going out. It was a Christmas present – he left it in my locker at school with an unsigned card. Romantic, right?'

'Are you sure it was him?' Alfie asks.

'Had to be,' I shrug. 'He never talked about it, but . . . who else would it be?'

'Who else?' he echoes sadly. 'Obviously . . .'

'Anyhow, I'm through with romance,' I tell him. 'I'm going to concentrate on my career instead. I mean . . . it's

165

just hormones, shaking us all up, causing trouble, wrecking everything. Girls want love and stuff, boys want . . . well, boys want something else.'

'Not always,' Alfie argues. 'Not all boys are like Aaron. And not all girls are looking for love either.'

I think of Honey, who flutters from one boy to the next like a butterfly moving from flower to flower. I think she might be looking for love actually. She's just looking in all the wrong places.

'Whichever way you look at it, growing up sucks,' I say. 'It's like some joke nature plays on us, the whole stupid mess of it.'

Through the trees we can see kids dancing in the flickering lantern light. We can hear the bass beat of the music, laughter, squeals, chat.

'It might seem that way sometimes,' Alfie says. 'Anthony is mad about your sister, isn't he? And she just sees him as a friend. Smart, useful . . . but just a friend. That's gotta hurt.'

'Surely he can see she's not interested, though? He needs to accept that.'

'Not easy, when you're mad about someone,' Alfie points out.

'I suppose. How about you then? Are you crushing on anyone?' I ask. 'Millie maybe?'

'No way!' he protests.

'You seemed to like her back in February, at the birthday party Skye and I had?'

Alfie is indignant. 'She jumped me!' he argues. 'One minute I was walking across the dance floor, the next she had me in a headlock. Well, a lip-lock actually. She's fiercer than she looks!'

I laugh.

'Millie is great, don't get me wrong,' Alfie says. 'But I like someone else . . .'

I bite my lip. 'Is it . . . is it Skye?' I ask. 'Because you've been spending a lot of time with her lately. Until Finch arrived on the scene anyhow.'

'It's not Skye,' he says.

'Tia?' I guess. 'Am I warm?'

Alfie shakes his head. 'Stone cold,' he sighs. 'Miles out.'

'Well, who then?'

Silence falls between us like a curtain, a wall.

'C'mon, spill!' I tease, elbowing him in the ribs, but Alfie just shrugs and stares out across the garden, refusing to meet my gaze. Something like fear begins to unfurl inside me. Suddenly, I don't want to know the answer. I really don't.

'She doesn't know,' Alfie whispers. 'She has no idea.'

Maybe she is just starting to work it out.

'What if she doesn't feel the same way about you?' I whisper. 'What if she's not looking for a relationship?'

'I'll wait,' he answers. 'I want her to know that. I'll wait, for as long as it takes.'

My face floods with colour in the darkness.

'Maybe . . . maybe she just sees you as a friend?'

'Maybe,' Alfie shrugs. 'Maybe she just doesn't see me at all.'

He jumps down from the trampoline and walks away through the trees, leaving me shell-shocked. I think back to that time in the school dinner queue, aged five, when Alfie asked me to be his girlfriend and then spoiled it all by blowing a raspberry in my ear. What if he really did like me? What if he still does?

Skye comes out of the darkness, hand in hand with Finch. 'Hey,' she says. 'We've been looking for you everywhere. It's nearly eleven, and that's our curfew. Coco went a while ago, she's staying at Linzi's in the village, and Shay's walked Cherry home already . . .'

My twin leaves something unspoken. 'So . . . what's up?' I ask, sliding down from the trampoline.

'Honey is what's up,' Skye says. 'She won't come home . . . she says Grandma Kate won't mind if she stays over. I've told her she has to come, but she won't listen to me. We promised Mum, Summer – Honey promised!'

Of course Skye doesn't know the half of it. I'm certain Honey has been sneaking out after curfew, probably to be with JJ. I lie awake at night and I hear every movement, every squeak of the floorboards. My big sister is kicking over the traces again.

'I'll talk to her,' I sigh.

Honey is holding court beneath an apple tree hung with tea-light lanterns, JJ's arm twined round her waist. I tug at her sleeve. 'Honey – it's almost eleven, time to go!'

'Go?' she echoes. 'Why? Will I turn into a pumpkin?'

'It's our curfew,' I remind her. 'Grandma Kate's expecting us back, and Mum made us promise . . .'

Honey untangles herself from JJ and pulls me into the shadows. 'Look, Summer, I'm not going home yet,' she says.

'I was grounded for months . . . I'm going to make the most of my freedom now! We're not little kids, you know! Make an excuse for me. Tell Grandma Kate I'm staying with a friend.'

I frown. 'What friend?' I ask, and Honey rolls her eyes.

'I'm staying here, stupid,' she says. 'The party's just starting! I'll sleep on the sofa. Anthony won't mind . . .'

Just like he doesn't mind her using his house as party central while she flirts with every cute boy in a five-mile radius, I think, but I daren't say the words out loud. Sometimes I think my sister has a cruel streak.

'Honey,' I plead. 'Grandma Kate will worry . . .'

'Not if you tell her I'm staying at a friend's,' Honey says crisply. 'Coco's sleeping at a mate's house, why not me? Just don't tell her it's a boy-mate!'

I bite my lip. 'Please don't make me lie for you!'

'Don't think of it as lying,' she says smoothly. 'More as doing me a favour. And in return . . . well, I won't mention how you're on some kind of starvation diet. Seriously, Summer, did you think nobody would notice? What are you playing at?'

'I don't know what you're talking about!'

❁ ❁

'I bet you don't,' Honey says, grabbing on to my wrist to stop me walking away. 'Well, fine. We'll talk about it with Grandma Kate instead . . .'

'Don't tell her,' I beg. 'Honey, please . . . it's just for another week, until the audition.'

'It had better be,' my sister says. 'Or I'll be ringing Mum in Peru to tell her what you're doing. You're crazy, Summer! You don't need to lose weight – you're a twig already. You'll make yourself ill!'

'You don't understand!'

Honey's face is cold. 'No, I don't,' she says. 'Summer, I'm not going to stay quiet about this for long, so get your act together. I won't mention your stupid diet and you'll tell Grandma Kate I'm staying with a friend. Deal?'

Her fingers dig into my wrist, but I break away and run through the darkened garden towards Skye and Finch.

'Is she coming?' my twin asks.

I shake my head, and Skye bites her lip. Honey is skidding off the rails again, and there's nothing we can do about it. My big sister has led me into a trap, one I can't wriggle out of.

I can't quite shake off the feeling of betrayal.

23

The next day I make strawberry cupcakes while Grandma Kate works alongside me, making steak pie. Baking is a kind of self-torture, a punishment. I know I cannot allow myself to eat the cupcakes, but there is a strange pleasure to be had from measuring out the ingredients for the sponge, spooning the batter into pretty cupcake cases, breathing in the warm, sweet aroma as they bake. I beat butter and sugar and vanilla essence together to make the frosting and pipe it carefully on, topping each one with a strawberry half.

My belly growls and my mouth waters, but I do not weaken. Last night I lied for Honey, and Grandma Kate didn't question me. I wish it hadn't been so easy.

My big sister slopes home at two in the afternoon with a

❀❀❀❀❀❀❀❀❀❀❀❀❀❀❀❀❀❀❀❀

bunch of hedgerow flowers she's picked along the lane, charming Grandma Kate in a heartbeat.

'Thank you, Honey!' she says, taking the flowers. 'You girls . . . it's such a treat to have this time with you, it really is! And you've been no trouble. Although it would be lovely if you could let me know first if you're planning to stay over with a friend, Honey, just so I know exactly where you are . . .'

'I'm so sorry, Grandma Kate,' Honey says, wide-eyed. 'I didn't think . . .'

'Well. No harm done . . .'

Honey shoots me a smug look and scoops up a cupcake, biting into warm yellow sponge and thick pink buttercream. I shudder. The cake is beautiful, perfect, deadly. I realize I am actually afraid of it.

'Want some?' she challenges me, waving the cake in front of my face. 'You made them, aren't you going to eat one?'

'Sure,' I say. 'I was going to take a book out to the hammock . . . and a cake.'

Honey laughs. 'But will you eat it?' she asks slyly. 'Or will you just feed it to Fred? He's been getting a little bit chubby lately, don't you think, Grandma Kate? As if someone's been giving him extras?'

173

If I had the courage, I'd reach out and slap Honey. Maybe I am feeding my food to Fred the dog, but that's my business, nobody else's.

'He looks just the same as always,' I say through gritted teeth.

'If you say so,' Honey shrugs, taking a second cupcake.

'Don't spoil your appetite,' I snap. 'We've got steak pie for tea, and there'll be chips . . .'

'Is Grandma Kate feeding you up?' Honey asks, fixing me with a dark look. 'About time. All that gorgeous flaky pastry and juicy steak. If you actually eat it, that is!'

'Of course she'll eat it!' Grandma Kate says. 'She's been helping me, haven't you, Summer? It'll be a real feast!'

Honey just raises one eyebrow, and I glare at her.

'We had a deal, remember?' I hiss when Grandma Kate's back is turned.

Honey laughs. 'My lips are sealed!'

Hurt twists inside me, raw and ugly. I love my big sister, but lately, I do not understand her. She is beautiful and funny and kind and clever, but she has a darker side too, a side that is mean and crazy and cruel. Right now, I don't know how to handle that. It feels far worse than anything

Aaron could say to me, worse than any criticisms Miss Elise could offer. It cuts me to the bone.

I know Honey's still hurting about Mum and Dad's split – she's made that clear, right from the start. But she acts like she's the only one who cares, and that's not fair. It's just that some of us keep the feelings hidden.

With Mum away, Honey is out of control again. She is pushing at the boundaries, pushing her luck. And this time, instead of Cherry or Paddy, or Mum – she's got it in for me.

By teatime, I am in my room, running through my barre exercises with one hand on the window sill. I told Grandma Kate that I wasn't hungry, that my head was hurting, my stomach aching, and both are actually true. My head hurts with the stress of trying to hide my food choices from people who won't understand; from pleasing Miss Elise, being ready for the audition; from trying to look as though life is good when actually it's crumbling away beneath my feet. My stomach aches because I am hungry, and because fear and anxiety churn around inside me endlessly.

I'd like to curl up under the duvet and sleep and sleep until the whole mess goes away, but I can't give up now.

Just a little more, the voice in my head cajoles. *You can do it, I know you can.*

The voice is encouraging for once, even though it is encouraging me to do something that hurts, exhausts. Still, I can't help trying to gain its approval. I go on dancing until the light fades, until I am too exhausted to stand.

24

At dance class on Sunday, Jodie watches me warily, like I have a terminal illness or something. She arrives early, like me, to practise before our lesson with Miss Elise, and catches me pulling on my leotard.

Her eyes register shock, concern, but I'm not fooled. Jodie is jealous. She can see I have lost weight, and it's a threat to her. She'd do anything to stop me losing more because it makes her look bad . . . and because she knows that if Sylvie Rochelle has to make a choice between a curvy girl and a slim one, she would have to choose the slim one.

Wouldn't she?

The trouble is I haven't quite lost enough. My thighs still seem huge in the regulation white tights and my hips and bum are as big as ever. Too big.

I pull on the big T-shirt I wear to practise, over the top of my leotard. Miss Elise is strict about us sticking to the regulation leotard and tights during class, but for the extra lessons she is more relaxed. It's what we are doing, not how neatly we are dressed, that matters here.

'Summer?' Jodie says, but I turn my face away.

I never imagined the two of us would fall out, especially not over something like this. Sacrifices . . . I didn't think that would include my friends.

I walk through to the studio and start on my barre work, and by the time I've moved on to the dance itself I'm so absorbed I barely notice that Jodie hasn't come through. Well, good. I hope she feels bad about the way she's acting. She should.

Today I will tell Miss Elise that I have changed my mind about helping at the summer dance sessions next week. I feel bad about it, but I will need every single minute of practice before the audition if I am going to be good enough. Surely Miss Elise will understand?

Jodie and Sushila finally come in, and then Miss Elise is there, taking us through our paces. She watches me carefully, through narrowed eyes. She doesn't comment, but I know

I am dancing better than last time. I put every scrap of energy and feeling into it, and the stress and confusion of the last few weeks retreat. This is why I dance, why it matters so much to me. I need it the way I need air to breathe.

'Good girl, Summer,' Miss Elise says. 'Your expressive dance is getting there. Better. Much better.' After class, she calls me over.

'How are you coping?' she asks. 'All set for the audition?'

I grin. 'I can't wait,' I tell her. 'I am working hard, Miss Elise, I promise you. I won't let you down.'

The teacher frowns. 'I misjudged things a little last time,' she says. 'I suggested you weren't taking things seriously, working hard enough. I can see that you are. I'm wondering now if perhaps you're pushing yourself a little too hard?'

'Too hard?' I echo, as if I don't quite understand the concept. I am not sure I do. The harder you work, the better you are, surely?

'You're using the studio here a lot more than usual, I know,' she says. 'We're very close to that audition now, Summer. You're step-perfect, and I want to make sure you keep the freshness, the energy I know you're capable of.'

❀❀❀❀❀❀❀❀❀❀❀❀❀❀❀❀❀❀❀❀❀

'Right . . .'

'So I want you to ease up on the practice,' Miss Elise says. 'Next week, the younger pupils are in for the summer sessions, and you said you'd help. You're so good with the little ones, Summer. I'd need you here all day, nine till four, looking after one of the groups . . .'

I panic. All of that time I could be practising, wasted . . . does Miss Elise want me to fail?

'Saturday's audition day!' I protest. 'Shouldn't I be focusing on that? I don't mind helping for a couple of hours a day, but . . .'

Miss Elise sighs. 'It would do you good to concentrate on something else for a while,' she says. 'Step back a little – get things into perspective.'

Perspective?

'Please?' Miss Elise persists. 'I was relying on you. And Jodie's helping . . .'

Well, Jodie would. How can I refuse, after all the time Miss Elise has spent on extra lessons? I fix on a smile. 'Fine, I'll do it. No problem.'

'One more thing,' Miss Elise says quietly. 'Some of your classmates seem to be worried about you, and now that I'm aware of it I'm concerned too. Your energy levels are very up and down lately. Have you been dieting?'

Anger bubbles up inside me. Jodie. Jealous, spiteful Jodie has been talking to Miss Elise – that's why she didn't come into the studio straight away. I tilt my chin, defiant.

'I'm eating well,' I tell her. 'I'm being careful – making healthy choices – that's all! What's wrong with that?'

Miss Elise sighs. 'You've lost weight, Summer; anyone can see that.'

Pride swells inside me, and a smile pulls at my lips. If Miss Elise can see it, Sylvie Rochelle will see it too.

'Promise me you'll stop this nonsense,' she says. 'Don't let me down.'

'I won't,' I promise.

Lately, though, I am finding that promises slip through my fingers like shards of melting ice, breaking into little pieces at my feet.

As it turns out, helping out at the summer school is not as bad as I imagined. My job is to take ten small girls in pink leotards from class to class, sampling jazz, ballet, tap and musical theatre. By the end of the week they will have learnt three new dances and an extract from a musical, complete with song.

On the first day, the kids swarm round me asking questions, begging for help with their hair or their shoes. I envy them their innocence. Back when I was seven or eight, I was just as bright-eyed. I had confidence and security, I knew where I belonged. My twin sister knew everything there was to know about me, and Mum was still married to Dad. I knew I was going to be a ballerina one day, up there on stage at the Royal Opera House, and I didn't even question it or think about how hard it might be to make it happen.

It's funny how things change. Confidence seeps away, families fall apart, twin sisters fall in love and don't have time for you any more. A dream can turn into a nightmare.

I don't say this to the kids, of course.

'Dance is a little bit of magic,' I tell them instead. 'It's as old as the human race. It's a way of saying things without words, of expressing ourselves, responding to the music. You need to work hard, though, to make the magic happen!'

'We will!' the kids promise.

One girl curls her hand round mine, peering up at me

❀❀❀❀❀❀❀❀❀❀❀❀❀❀❀❀❀❀❀❀❀

with wide green eyes. 'My name is Fern,' she says solemnly. 'When I'm grown up, I want to be just like you . . .'

No, you don't, I think. You really, really don't.

At breaktime I take them down to the dance school cafe for juice and biscuits and fruit; I pick at strawberries while they crunch on chocolate-chip cookies, and I remember the days when I had never heard of calories. I wish I could go back to that time.

At lunchtime the little ones sit down to sandwiches and crisps and ice cream. I have my own lunch: lettuce and tomatoes and tuna, a few segments of orange, a glass of water.

'Don't you want ice cream?' Fern asks, eyes wide. 'Don't you like it?'

'No . . . it's just . . . I'm trying to stay slim,' I explain awkwardly. 'I have a big audition on Saturday, for a really brilliant ballet school.'

Fern frowns. 'And . . . you can't eat ice cream any more?' she asks. 'I don't understand. Because you're thin already, ever so thin, Summer. You're just like a real ballerina!'

'Thank you,' I say, my cheeks flushing with pleasure. I hope the teachers on Saturday agree.

❀❀❀❀❀❀❀❀❀❀❀❀❀❀❀❀❀❀❀❀

Fern pushes her ice cream away, unfinished. 'I'd like to be thin too,' she says, looking down at her round little-girl tummy in the tight pink leotard, and I feel sick with shame.

'You're perfect just the way you are!' I argue. 'I promise. All of you are perfect! Eat up that ice cream!'

I push the dish back towards her, and she caves in instantly and scoops up a huge spoonful, laughing with her friends. What kind of a person am I, making a little girl feel like she can't eat ice cream? I would never want her to feel like she wasn't as good as anyone else. I would never want her to feel the way I feel inside, heavy, hopeless, hungry for something I can never have.

Across the dance school cafe, I watch Jodie sitting with her team, laughing as she decorates her ice cream with squiggles of sauce and sugar sprinkles. I shudder, but a part of me envies Jodie. She is chatting and smiling and eating ice cream, and I cannot honestly say that she looks big at all, just slim and pretty and happy. She looks at me and smiles, but I freeze out her grin with a frosty glare.

You don't need her, the voice in my head insists. *Look at her, stuffing her face! It's disgusting!*

I push my Tupperware box of salad away.

25

At four o'clock, when the workshops end and the kids are collected by mums, dads and grannies, I head for the senior ballet studio to put in some practice on my expressive dance.

Every step is perfect, every move smooth and streamlined. I dance and stretch and whirl and leap, but no matter how hard I try, I cannot lose myself in the music. I feel as though I am going through the motions, following a formula I know off by heart. I could do this dance in my sleep, yet I cannot bring it to life. The harder I try, the further away the magic seems to be.

Will the judges notice at my audition on Saturday? They are looking for perfection, technical excellence, and I think I can deliver that. They are also looking for something extra – potential, expression, emotion, life. I used to be able to do that too, but lately, those qualities have deserted me.

No wonder I am afraid. My dream of becoming a dancer is turning into a nightmare.

By the time I come out of the final spin in my last dance, I am exhausted, shaking with the effort of trying to push past 'perfect' and find my spark.

'Summer?'

Miss Elise's voice cuts into my thoughts, and I turn to see my teacher standing in the studio doorway. She doesn't look impressed. 'This just isn't you,' she says. 'Like I said last week, you're working too hard. I can't fault you technically, but . . . something's been lost.'

My heart feels as if it is breaking in two. Miss Elise sees the look on my face and sighs. 'I'm sorry, Summer.' She moves towards me and slips an arm round my shoulders, comforting, kind, but abruptly I feel her recoil. I see shock run through her, and something like revulsion.

'Oh, Summer,' she says. 'You're skin and bone! Would you take off the T-shirt? You've been hiding away under that thing for weeks now.'

I bite my lip. I really don't want to take off the T-shirt

because then Miss Elise will see that even if I have lost some weight, I still have a lot more to go. I cross my arms around my body, awkward, defensive.

'The T-shirt?' she prompts.

Turning away, I peel it off and stand huddled in my leotard. I feel like a beached whale, exposed, heavy, hopeless.

'Good grief,' Miss Elise says. 'You're wasting away . . .'

I see the shock in her eyes, hear the words, but all I can feel is a tidal wave of elation. I am in control. I've spent the last few weeks starving, my belly aching with hunger, mouth watering as my sisters tucked into strawberry cupcakes and pizza and cheesecake, without tasting so much as a mouthful myself. I have proved that I am strong, determined. I have changed the way I look, and it shows.

I look in the studio mirror. I catch a glimpse of a willowy girl with shadowed blue eyes, pale skin, fair hair pinned in neat braids around her head. She is slender, childlike. You can see her ribs through the stretchy fabric of the leotard; her hip bones jut sharply and her stomach is concave, hollowed out. Then the image changes. The mirror seems to warp as I watch, buckling and rippling like the fairground Hall of Mirrors on the film set.

187

❀❀❀❀❀❀❀❀❀❀❀❀❀❀❀❀❀❀❀❀❀❀

My heart sinks. The girl staring back at me is huge, loathsome, a fat blob in a leotard. Salty tears roll down my cheeks, one after another, and I don't seem to be able to stop them.

'Summer,' Miss Elise is saying. 'Can you hear me? You need to start eating. And I want you to stop practising too – I mean it. You're pushing yourself too hard.'

Don't listen, don't listen, don't listen! the voice inside my head screams.

'You'll make yourself ill,' Miss Elise is saying. 'I know what you're doing, and trust me, it's a very dangerous game.'

'It's not a game,' I whisper.

She sighs. 'No, it's really not. But whatever it is, you need to stop it, right now. Do I have to call your mother and discuss all of this with her?'

'Mum's in Peru,' I say flatly.

'Of course – the honeymoon. Well . . . your grandma then? Should I be talking to her?'

I take a deep breath in and wipe the tears away. I square my shoulders, look Miss Elise in the eye.

'I am not dieting,' I lie. 'And I'm not ill, I promise you. I'm just a bit stressed about the audition. Perhaps I've been

❀❀❀❀❀❀❀❀❀❀❀❀❀❀❀❀❀❀❀

exercising too much, cutting out too many treat foods, but only because I want this so much. I really, really do.'

'I know,' my teacher says softly. 'But, Summer, this isn't the right way to go about it.'

What does she know? the voice in my head rages. *She's trying to stop you, spoil it all . . .*

But Miss Elise is my teacher. She has always supported me, pushed me, encouraged me. She has always told me that she believes in me. Why would she sabotage me now? My head aches with confusion.

'Summer, you have a very real talent for dance,' Miss Elise says gently. 'That's special. But this pressure . . . the worry of the audition . . . you've let the stress and worry of it all get to you.'

'I haven't!' I protest. 'I'm fine!'

The teacher shakes her head. 'You are a gifted dancer, but I'm not sure that residential ballet school would be the best thing for you at the moment. It's not right for everyone. It's a high-stress career, and unless you're strong . . .'

'I am strong!' I whisper. 'I can handle it! The pressure, the worry – it's fine, Miss Elise; it's just spurring me on to work harder!'

Thoughts race through my head, disastrous, dreadful thoughts. Miss Elise and Sylvie Rochelle are friends. Suppose my dance teacher tells Sylvie Rochelle I am not cut out for a career in dance? Success or failure for me could hinge on her words, her views.

'I want this scholarship place more than anything!' I plead. 'You have to understand! Please don't tell me it's not right for me! Don't tell Sylvie Rochelle I'm not good enough!'

Miss Elise frowns. 'Of course I'll support you, and I would never tell Sylvie you weren't good enough – you are, that's not in doubt,' she says. 'I'm just asking you to think about it some more, that's all. Is this really what you want? This level of pressure and anxiety, all through your life? Because ballet is not an easy career to follow, Summer.'

'I know that!'

'Few dancers are talented enough to make a living from it,' Miss Elise says. 'Those that do are signing up for a world of hard work, punishing schedules, rejection. It's not all bouquets of flowers and feathered tutus, and it's a very short career, even for the best dancers . . .'

'I know all that!' I repeat. 'Are you saying I'm not good enough? Are you saying I don't have what it takes?'

But I don't hear any more because I am running by then, out of the dance studio, grabbing up my ballet bag, then out of the building. I don't look back.

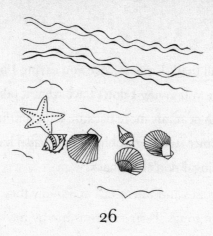

26

I turn up as usual the next day because I don't want to let the little kids down, but I stay away from Miss Elise.

I used to trust her. I used to think she was the coolest person I knew. A few words of praise from her would put me on cloud nine, once upon a time, but now I know what she really thinks. That I am weak, lazy, liable to crack under the pressure of being at dance school. Oh, and fat too, because when she tried to comfort me yesterday there was no way on earth she could have thought I was really 'skin and bone'. That must have been a cruel joke because I know I am as big as ever.

I blank out the thought and put all my energy into working with the kids. I am getting to know them now, to see their strengths and weaknesses, their personalities, even a little slice of their hopes and dreams. I take extra time with Fern, trying to boost her confidence, helping her with her steps and routines.

In musical theatre, the classes are working towards putting on a performance from *Annie*. Yesterday the group did drama exercises and warm-ups and today they are singing some of the songs. Fern surprises me by having a sweet, clear voice that grabs the teacher's attention. 'Good,' he tells her. 'Shoulders back, take a deep breath and let the singing come from deep inside you. Great stuff!'

Fern's cheeks are pink and she glows with pride.

The next day the group starts to put together a routine around one of the songs, with some dancing and acting and lots of singing. It's cool to see the routine come together, and encouraging to see that every girl has different strengths. Some are good at acting, some at dance, some at singing. Fern is shy, but when she sings, she shines, and at the end of the lesson the teacher tells her he's picked her out of all the kids in the summer school groups to take the part of Annie.

Her eyes widen. 'Really? Me? Are you sure?'

'Certain,' I tell her. 'We need the best person for the job. And that's you!'

'I'll do it then,' she says, determined. 'If you think I can.'

As the class file out afterwards, the teacher stops me. I am on my guard at once. Is he about to nag me about my weight too? Has Miss Elise told him to keep an eye on me?

Maybe not.

'You're very good with those kids,' he says. 'I'm teaching all the groups so I've seen the other student helpers, and you're far and away the best of them. You put so much in. You care. You bring out the best in kids, build their confidence. That's a talent in itself, you know. Thanks!'

'Oh . . . no worries,' I reply. 'It's fun.' And I realize that it is.

This week really has given me something else to think about apart from the audition. It's always there, of course, looming at the back of my mind, but just for a while, each day, I get to focus on the good stuff about dance, not the stressy stuff. I get to remember why I loved it so much.

Correction: why I still do love it so much.

Once I am back at Tanglewood, though, the panic starts. I don't trust Miss Elise's judgement any more, but still,

I am afraid to disobey her. I can't risk messing up my audition.

Forbidden from practising, I am going stir-crazy. I make a quiche laden with cheese and cream and two trays of chocolate brownies that smell like heaven. I do not take a single bite. I mop the hallway and kitchen, tidy the living room and generally bug Grandma Kate. 'You'll wear yourself out,' she warns me. 'That's no good – Saturday's your big day, remember?'

As if I could forget.

You'll fail, the voice in my head tells me. *You haven't worked hard enough. You're not good enough . . .*

I push out of the kitchen and walk across the garden, down the cliff steps and on to the deserted beach. It is probably too late to swim, and I am scared to wade into the water because I am out of my depth already, even on dry land. If I started swimming, the temptation to head straight for the horizon would be too much.

Instead, I turn and run along the sand, each step helping to silence the nagging voice inside me. I run until my head is empty, my body weary, my muscles aching. The light is fading as I turn and run back again, pushing myself, punishing my body, trying to find some peace.

❀❀❀❀❀❀❀❀❀❀❀❀❀❀❀❀❀❀❀❀❀

As I reach the cliff steps, I see a hunched figure sitting on a rock at the bottom, looking out at the ocean.

'Alfie?' I say, startled. 'What're you doing here?'

'Just passing,' he quips.

'Yeah, right.'

'OK,' he shrugs. 'I just thought I'd swing by. Wish you luck, or break a leg or whatever people say, for the audition on Saturday. And you weren't home, so I thought I'd do some sunbathing. And now even the sun's given up on me . . .'

I sink down on to the warm sand, glad to rest and gather my breath. 'I went for a run,' I tell Alfie. 'Trying to take my mind off it. But . . . well, thanks for the thought.'

'It's not that I want you to actually break a leg obviously,' he says. 'I just hope . . . well, I hope it turns out the way you want it to. Even if it does mean you moving away. You'll come home for holidays, right?'

'Of course,' I say. 'Obviously I will.'

It's strange, though. I have poured so much energy and effort into working for this audition, yet sometimes I can barely remember why I want it so badly. I try to picture the glossy wooden floors and shiny, mirrored studios of Rochelle Academy from the brochure, but they slide out of reach like distant memories, too vague to recall. It's as if a whole part of my mind has been wiped clean, leaving me struggling to remember just what I am working for.

Which is kind of terrifying.

'I'll miss you,' Alfie says into the darkness. 'Who else could squash me flat with one glance when I try some dodgy practical joke at school? Who else would dare tell me not to wear eyeliner in public? Only you, Summer Tanberry!' He laughs, but it's a sad kind of laugh.

'I haven't always been very nice to you, have I?'

'Don't be daft,' Alfie says. 'You've always been . . . well, lovely. Harsh sometimes, yes, but . . . well, I expect I deserved it!'

Lovely? I am not sure it's even possible that Alfie Anderson could say such a thing about me, but somehow, in the dark, the words don't seem so scary.

'Maybe we just didn't get each other,' I shrug. 'I thought you were loud and clueless and cheesy. Always trying to wind me up . . .'

'I am all of those things,' he admits. 'I wasn't trying to wind you up, though. I was only ever trying to get your attention.'

Even though I cannot see in the shadowy light, I know Alfie's cheeks will be flushed with pink. This is what he was trying to tell me at the party – he has liked me all along. The endless pranks and teasing were just a way to make me notice him. And I never really did until now, when he dropped the jokes and grew up a little. Better late than never, I guess.

I know what it is like to try and try and try to capture someone's attention. It's what I used to do with Dad, when I was little. Growing up in a family of four sisters, it was hard to stand out, but dancing gave me a chance to do that.

'Hey,' Dad used to say, watching me skip round the living room in a pink net skirt at the age of five. 'How's my little ballerina?'

Keeping his attention was impossible, though, especially after he and Mum split. I can still feel the hurt of that in my chest, an ache, an emptiness.

'I'm an idiot, right?' Alfie says sadly.

'No, you're a mate,' I tell him, hoping it doesn't sound too cruel.

I am not looking for another boyfriend, but I realize that Alfie is a true friend. He is kind and loyal, and he has a knack of being around when I need him. That's more than I can say for Tia or Millie lately, or even Skye . . . I have pushed them all away, made myself too busy with practice, and they have allowed it to happen. It's only Alfie who has refused to be discouraged.

'OK then,' he sighs. 'Speaking as a mate – I'm worried, Summer. This diet thing. Healthy eating, whatever. It stops once the audition is over, yeah?'

'Definitely,' I say, and then all my certainty drains away. 'I think so anyway. I hope so. Maybe. I don't know, Alfie . . . I just can't seem to help it.'

'Talk to somebody,' he says. 'Your mum, your gran, your dad, a doctor. It's getting scary. It's getting out of hand, and I don't know what to do.'

I guess that makes two of us.

27

That night I am changing out of my T-shirt and joggers when Skye walks into the bedroom and catches me in my bra and knickers. The smile freezes on her face and although I try to cover up quickly, I know it's too late. She has seen me, and she cannot hide her shock.

'Summer!' she whispers. 'What's going on? You're like a skeleton!'

'Don't be ridiculous,' I say calmly. 'I'm no different. Just a bit more . . . toned maybe. From all the extra dancing.'

'I could see your ribs!' Skye accuses. 'Your shoulder blades looked like they were about to slice through your skin! I know you're watching what you eat, but . . . this is scary, Summer! I had no idea!'

Because you've been so wrapped up with Finch, I think

meanly. Too busy falling in love to notice how lost, how frightened I am.

'I'm fine,' I lie. 'And I am eating, it's just that we're not sitting down to eat as a family any more. Everyone's busy, doing different things. Besides, I made the tea! I ate about four brownies while I was making them, I swear . . . It's just that I'm burning lots of energy from all that practice.'

Skye isn't fooled. She drags the T-shirt out of my hands. My eyes flicker up to the mirror, and for a second I see my reflection as Skye sees it: a ladder of ribs, the long ridge of my spine, shoulder blades jutting sharply, wing-like. I look pale, wasted, worn out.

'Stop it, Summer,' she whispers. 'Please? You have to stop this.'

Don't listen, the voice wheedles. *She doesn't understand – none of them do. You still have a long way to go. Trust me . . . I'm on your side.*

'Back off,' I tell my sister harshly. 'I'm fine, Skye. I don't know what you're talking about.'

I cannot sleep. My head is a tangle of shadows and fears, my heart aches with sadness and a kaleidoscope of memories from long ago are whirling through my mind.

201

✿✿✿✿✿✿✿✿✿✿✿✿✿✿✿✿✿✿✿✿✿

I didn't think my own twin would turn against me, try to stop me from reaching my dream. Then I remember the look of shock on her face, and I wonder if I've got that wrong, if she's honestly just concerned. Would she understand?

'Skye?' I whisper into the darkness, but my twin just sighs and turns in her sleep, lost in dreams of vintage dresses and a boy called Finch.

I check my mobile. There's a message from Mum, telling me that she and Paddy are heading back to Lima, ready to fly home. She tells me to do my best on Saturday, that she is proud of me now and always, no matter what. My fingers hover over the call button for a long moment. If I could just talk to Mum right now . . .

But I can't. What would I say? 'Hey, Mum, my life is falling apart. I'm scared to eat and I can't dance and my dreams are in pieces around my feet, so don't be proud of me . . . I'm a mess.'

I don't think so. And if not Mum, not Skye, then who?

I snap the mobile closed and slide out of bed, shivering a little, and pad downstairs. There is no sound in the kitchen except the slow ticking of the clock, the hum of the Aga and the sound of Fred the dog snuffling as he settles in his basket in the corner and chases imaginary rabbits in his head.

It is past two o'clock, but Dad's bit of Australia is ten hours ahead of us. We Skype him every Christmas and birthday, but I have not actually called my dad since the year he left, when Skye and I went down to the call box in Kitnor to plead with him to come home because Coco was crying and Honey was raging and Mum's smile was so brittle we thought she might shatter into a thousand pieces at any minute. Dad told us to stop worrying, that it was all for the best, that he still loved us even though he wasn't living with us any more.

That was the day we knew we'd really lost him, the day we understood that he was never coming home again.

I find Mum's address book in the dresser drawer and tap out the code and number for Dad in Australia. The line connects and Dad's voice fills the silence, muffled, distant, slightly annoyed.

'Hello? Charlotte, is that you? I'm at work, for God's sake!'

'It's me,' I whisper. 'Summer. I wanted to talk to you!'

✿✿✿✿✿✿✿✿✿✿✿✿✿✿✿✿✿✿✿✿✿✿

'Summer!' he says, as if trying to place me. 'Summer? Is something wrong?'

No, Dad, nothing's wrong. It's two in the morning and I am scared because my life is falling to bits, but no, nothing's wrong. I don't say this, of course.

'I just wanted to talk,' I say lamely.

'Well . . . that's very nice, Summer, but I'm pretty busy right now. Was there something in particular?'

I swallow hard. It feels like there is a lump the size of a golf ball in my throat, stopping me from speaking, breathing.

'No, no . . . I just wanted to tell you I have my audition on Saturday. For the dance school. And I'm a bit . . . um . . . nervous.'

Far away, on the other side of the world, I can hear Dad talking to someone else, giving orders, asking for a report to be on his desk within the hour.

'Sorry about that,' he says. 'It's chaos here. So you're in a new dance show, is that it? Don't worry, you'll be brilliant as usual. My little ballerina.'

A tear rolls down my cheek, salty, silent. He couldn't even be bothered to listen properly.

❀❀❀❀❀❀❀❀❀❀❀❀❀❀❀❀❀❀❀❀

'OK,' I say. 'Right. Dad, I have to go now. Someone's calling me.'

'No worries, take care, do your best!'

'I will,' I promise.

The line goes dead.

Friday goes by in a blur. The morning is filled with rehearsals and the afternoon with the dance show itself, so I am kept busy running around making sure my team is OK. Kelsey forgets her tap shoes and Rowan's leotard splits along one seam and Fern's curly Annie wig keeps slipping down over one eye, but with the help of borrowed shoes and last-minute stitching and several heavy-duty hairgrips, everything is perfect for the performance.

As Fern and the rest of the team take their bows at the end, I clap and cheer louder than any of the parents, my heart filled with pride and happiness. It is the most alive I have felt in weeks.

Back home, Grandma Kate has made omelette and salad and I eat almost a quarter of the omelette, Skye watching me like a hawk, before slipping the rest to Fred the minute she goes to the fridge for more lemonade.

'I want to come with you tomorrow,' she announces as we stack the dishwasher. 'What with Mum being away and everything. For moral support. OK?'

I look at her eyes, dark with reproach, and I am torn between regret and terror. Does she really care, or would she just force-feed me chocolate and milkshake on the car journey there? I can't risk that. Maybe she is worried, but it's too little, too late.

'It's not OK actually,' I say. 'Miss Elise is taking me. Let's just leave it at that.'

'Your mum asked me to go along,' Grandma Kate frowns. 'That was the plan, and I'd love to see this new dance school . . .'

'No,' I say firmly. 'I'll do this alone. I'm so nervous already I just wouldn't be able to hold it together if anyone else was there. I'm sorry – it's just that I need to focus.'

'I suppose,' Skye huffs. 'Anyway, we're planning a big beach barbie tomorrow night to celebrate . . . everyone's invited!'

'Big mouth,' Honey says with a roll of her eyes. 'That was meant to be a surprise!'

'What if there isn't anything to celebrate?' I protest, stricken. 'I might not find out how I've done for ages . . .'

✿✿✿✿✿✿✿✿✿✿✿✿✿✿✿✿✿✿✿✿

'We're celebrating the end of you practising every spare minute,' Skye says. 'And the end of you being stressed and wound up the whole time . . .'

'And the end of you eating like a sparrow,' Honey chips in. I shoot her a warning look, but she pretends not to notice.

'That too,' Skye says grimly, but Grandma Kate doesn't seem to hear.

'Don't worry, Summer,' she says. 'It will all be over by this time tomorrow.'

'I can't wait,' I sigh.

28

I am so nervous my hands are shaking and I have to tie and retie my new pointe shoes two or three times to get the ribbons right. I am in the changing rooms of Studio One at the Rochelle Academy, and the room is a crush of girls in leotards and white tights, chatting, laughing, checking their perfect hair.

I check my mobile. A message from Mum telling me she loves me, that she and Paddy are rooting for me; a message from Skye telling me to knock their socks off; a message from Alfie Anderson saying he got my number from Skye and wants to wish me luck.

I smile, in spite of myself.

Every ten minutes a stern-faced woman with a clipboard comes through to call somebody out into the studio. Ten

❁❁❁❁❁❁❁❁❁❁❁❁❁❁❁❁❁❁❁❁❁❁❁

minutes . . . is that all we get? Eight weeks of stress and worry and endless practice, so that our futures can be decided in ten minutes flat? Crazy.

'I am just so buzzed,' one girl says. 'Mum and I have travelled all the way from Birmingham . . .'

'It's an amazing opportunity,' another chips in. 'My dance teacher says that Rochelle Academy is set to become one of the most prestigious ballet schools in the country . . .'

I cannot imagine spending the next five years of my life with these girls; I can't even imagine spending the next five minutes of it with them.

'OK?' Jodie says into my ear, and I am so glad to see her that for a moment I struggle to remember why we're not friends any more.

'Not OK,' I whisper.

'Me neither,' she says. 'Talk about butterflies in my tummy – it's more like a herd of elephants.'

'I can't do this . . .'

Jodie takes hold of my hands. 'Summer Tanberry, you totally CAN. Yes, it's scary, but it's just an audition. We've practised, we know what to do . . . we'll be OK. This is just stage fright. It's normal!'

What does she know? the voice inside my head hisses. *Don't trust her!*

I take a deep breath in. 'Why are you being nice to me?' I ask.

Jodie sighs. 'Why wouldn't I be nice to you? We're friends, aren't we? At least we were. I'm sorry you're upset with me, but if I spoke to Miss Elise, it was only ever because I was worried about you, because I was trying to help . . .'

'I know,' I whisper. 'I'm sorry, Jodie.'

'It's just because I was worried,' she repeats, squeezing my hands. 'You're a brilliant dancer, Summer. Believe it. Get out there and show them!'

The stern-faced lady appears in the doorway, clipboard in hand. 'Summer Tanberry, please!'

Miss Elise and I follow her along a wood-panelled corridor hung with ballet prints. I falter and look more closely. I recognize them from an art book Mum showed me a couple of years ago, of an artist called Degas. I remember thinking at the time that he made the magic of dance come alive with a few strokes of pastel, but as I look now, all I can see are the dancers themselves.

They are strong and curvy, their shoulders muscled, legs

❀❀❀❀❀❀❀❀❀❀❀❀❀❀❀❀❀❀❀

sturdy, their bodies stocky and powerful. They are not waifs, not even close. My head clouds with confusion. Have I got it wrong somehow, all that stuff about shape and build? Surely not.

Ugly, the voice in my head says, but it seems quieter now, less certain. *Huge, hideous . . .*

'Summer?' Miss Elise asks gently. 'Are you OK?'

'Yes . . . yes, sure.'

But I am not OK, of course. I take one last look at the pictures, and I can see that those dancers are not huge or hideous or ugly. They're beautiful. What if everything I thought was right turns out to be wrong? Cold fear settles inside me, heavy as stone.

I don't know what I am doing here.

I know that the studio is big and light and airy, with a sweet scent of floor polish and resin and expectation. I know that there are three people seated behind a table at the far end of the studio, and that one of them is Sylvie Rochelle. I know that there is a cold sweat prickling the back of my neck as I walk across the shiny wooden floor into the centre of the room, and I know that my heart is beating so loudly it is a miracle nobody asks what the noise is.

I am afraid – of not being good enough or thin enough; of not having what it takes to be a dancer. I wonder if the voice is right, if I am wasting everybody's time here, my own included. The fear sinks down through my body like petrol soaking through dry grass, and I begin to dance.

I dance well. My barre exercises are good, my set piece strong, and then Miss Elise changes the CD and Stravinsky's wild music begins. I take a deep breath and the music takes hold of me, the way it used to, and I lose myself. I feel the flames leap through my body, crackling, burning – I dance with every bit of my heart and soul, with fear and hope and hunger. And all the time, the flames are raging, right inside me, burning me up.

There is no chance of Miss Elise or anyone else saying that I have no 'spark'. This dance is all spark, fireworks and flame, destructive, beautiful. When I finish, breathless, I look up and see the three judges looking at me wide-eyed, as if I have done something unexpected, unimagined, perhaps slightly scary.

Pink spots of shame begin to bloom in my cheeks as I

stand, shivering slightly now, beneath their gaze. Sylvie Rochelle is the first to speak.

'Summer,' she says. 'Thank you! I can see that you love to dance. Such energy, such emotion.'

I blink. Energy? Emotion? This seems unlikely to me. I feel empty, hollowed out, exhausted.

'So you can dance,' the man on Miss Rochelle's left says, peering over narrow glasses rimmed in red. 'But what else do you have to offer? What are your plans, your dreams?'

I open my mouth to explain that a chance like this is all I have ever wanted, all I have ever dreamt about, but the words are like gravel in my throat, sharp, painful.

Pathetic, the voice in my head says, braver now. *You could never fit in here. You're not good enough, not dedicated enough, not thin enough.*

'Summer?' the man prompts. 'Your hopes, your dreams?'

'I . . . I don't know,' I stammer, flustered.

He frowns. 'We have just three scholarship places to award. Can you tell me why you think we should give one of them to you?'

I search around for reasons. There used to be a million and one of them – my future was all mapped out, bright

❀❀❀❀❀❀❀❀❀❀❀❀❀❀❀❀❀❀❀

and shiny and successful. I have worked so hard the last few weeks to make it real. I have pushed myself to breaking point, or maybe beyond it, but right now, I cannot find one single good reason why anyone would give a scholarship place to me.

Silence fills the studio, heavy and ominous. In the corner, I can see Miss Elise covering her face with one hand, as if giving up on me. 'Are you eating properly?' the woman on Sylvie Rochelle's right asks. 'You are very thin. This is a pressured environment, a pressured career. You need a good sense of self-worth to handle it all. We cannot take girls who starve themselves in a misguided attempt to fit in – we're looking for dancers who are strong, both physically and mentally.'

'I am eating fine,' I protest. 'I am strong! I'm just . . . naturally . . .'

Gross, I think. *Big. Chunky, meaty, fat, solid.* But when I look in the mirror I know that's not the reality.

'. . . slim,' I finish.

In your dreams, the voice taunts me, but I push it away.

I glance across at Miss Elise, who looks stricken. I have blown it, I can see. Everything I ever wanted is falling through my fingers, and there's nothing I can do to stop it.

214

'I eat healthily, most of the time,' I say in a cool, clear voice. 'But . . . well, my parents run a chocolate business, so I do get tempted sometimes. Nobody's perfect. I'm just lucky, I guess. No matter what I eat, I don't put on weight.'

The lies drip off my tongue so easily I surprise even myself. I can see Miss Elise, her eyebrows raised, her mouth a perfect circle of surprise.

'I need this place,' I go on. 'It's my dream. I have worked hard for this, but it hasn't felt like work because I've loved every minute. I am strong, I promise you, much stronger than I look. Give me a chance. I want to dance – I want to lose myself in the music, feel it with my heart and soul. I want to be a dancer more than anything else in the world.'

I smile then, my best stage smile, sparkling, bright.

The adults talk quietly together, and then Sylvie Rochelle turns to me. 'Thank you,' she says. 'That will be all for now. Letters will be sent out next week to confirm which of you have been offered a place, but . . .'

Her face softens and she smiles at me. 'I think we can safely say that it will be good news for you, Summer. You're a natural.'

The floor shifts a little beneath my feet and for a moment

I think I may fall. I don't, though. I stand tall, my shoulders back, my chin tilted high.

'Thank you,' I say shakily. 'Thank you! You don't know what this means to me!'

Sylvie Rochelle smiles. 'I think I can guess.'

29

My family are good at celebrations. When Miss Elise drops me back at Tanglewood that afternoon, someone has dug out the wedding bunting and hung it all around the garden and my little sister Coco is sitting in a tree playing the music from *Swan Lake*, very badly, on her violin. It's painful, but it makes me smile.

'Your mum will be proud,' Grandma Kate tells me. 'We're ALL so proud, Summer!'

'It's not definite,' I remind them. 'I won't believe it until I see it on paper, in black and white . . .'

'It sounded pretty definite to me,' Skye says. She hugs me tight and I don't care any more about Finch because I love my twin, always, no matter what.

I am lucky, I know, a hundred times luckier than I deserve.

Neither Jodie nor Sushila were told they could expect good news, so I kept quiet about what Sylvie Rochelle had said to me. To boast about it would have felt like tempting fate, and besides, I can't help feeling sad for Jodie and Sushila. They wanted a place as much as I did.

'One of them may still be lucky,' Miss Elise mused in the car driving home while Jodie and Sushila travelled back with their families. 'It's always possible. Jodie danced really well.'

I remember Jodie's kindness earlier, and I wonder how I ever thought she hated me, was jealous, wanted me to fail. I think perhaps I got that wrong. But at the end of the day, Sylvie Rochelle had the choice between a slim girl and a curvy girl, and she chose . . . me. I didn't fail . . . not this time.

My future is opening out before me, the way I always dreamt it would. I should be jumping up and down with excitement, but somehow I feel flat and numb and empty. I need time to take it in.

This audition will change my life. From now on I will live and breathe ballet, from morning to night. If I think I have worked hard to get to this point, I know I will need to work harder still to stay there. Suddenly, that knowledge feels heavy, stifling. Whatever Skye and Alfie think, this audition doesn't mean the end of practising every chance I can, but the start of stepping things up to a whole new level.

It won't be the end of dieting either. One of the panellists called me 'very thin', and now that phrase is lodged in my head. A glow of pride warms me whenever I think of it, even though I am not totally sure it can be true. If I am thin, I need to make sure I go on looking that way . . . and that means being careful about what I eat.

We have a picnic tea on the lawn. I eat most of a hard-boiled egg and some salad leaves, and then Grandma Kate brings out a cake iced with white chocolate buttercream and topped with strawberries and edged with the Summer's Dream truffles Paddy invented for my thirteenth birthday. The sight of it makes my stomach growl with hunger and my heart race with panic.

The cake is beautiful, but it scares me. There's no way on earth I want to even touch it.

'It's lovely, but I'm full,' I argue. 'I just couldn't . . .'

'You ate one boiled egg and a couple of lettuce leaves,' Honey says harshly. 'So yes, actually, you could.'

'Grandma Kate made it,' Coco chips in. 'Especially for you!'

Honey looks angry, but Skye's eyes are scared. 'Summer,' she says softly. 'Come on. Just one slice.'

So I cut the smallest slice ever, my hands shaking. I do not want to taste it, but I cannot drop it and run away, no matter how much I'd like to. I take a bite, and the rich, sweet icing melts in my mouth. It's good, better than good. I take a second bite.

How could something that tastes so good be so bad? Have I somehow got this wrong? This is a cake made with love and pride by my grandma, decorated with the truffles Paddy created for me using my favourite strawberries and cream filling. Can that really be so awful?

It's like a drug, the voice in my head hisses. *Are you going to let it unravel all your hard work? Have you no willpower at all?*

I put the slice of cake down.

'Hey,' Skye whispers. 'Don't worry. You did OK.'

The beach party that night is the best one yet. Grandma Kate has extended our curfew to midnight and my sisters have invited everyone within a five-mile radius, even

Anthony. Finch is still dressed as a gypsy boy after the day's latest filming; he and Skye look like they were made for each other. Coco and her friends are fussing over Humbug, who has been brought down to the party specially from her home in one of the old stables. A whole bunch of film crew people are here, including Chris and Marty and some girls I remember vaguely from the props and make-up departments.

Honey comes over to me, slipping an arm round my waist like I am her favourite person in the whole world. My big sister is mercurial, shiny one moment and bright and blazing the next, but lately, I just find her mood swings exhausting, infuriating.

'This is our last chance to have fun,' she shrugs. 'Live a little. Tomorrow night Mum and Paddy will be home and we'll have no freedom at all . . .'

I roll my eyes. Mum and Paddy give us plenty of freedom, but it could never be enough for Honey. Sometimes I think she is actually looking for rules to break.

'Anyway, we're celebrating! Here's to my little sister, the famous ballerina!' Honey hands me a paper cup of something fizzy and apple-ish.

❀❀❀❀❀❀❀❀❀❀❀❀❀❀❀❀❀❀

'Drink it,' she says. 'It's only a cider shandy! Not even very strong!'

'I can't!' I say. 'I'm thirteen, Honey! What are you playing at?'

Her eyes narrow. 'I'm trying to loosen you up,' she says. 'Relax you a little bit. Is that a crime? You're wound up so tight these days you'll snap any minute. I've been watching you, Summer. You practise every hour of the day – that's not passion, it's obsession. And you're frightened to eat, which is crazy because you're wasting away . . .'

Her eyes soften, suddenly sad. 'You're a mess, Summer, and trust me, I know what that feels like. It takes one to know one.'

Anger pulses in my throat. My big sister Honey is beautiful and talented, but her life is a car crash, chaotic, disastrous. She lives so close to the edge she is in constant danger of falling, and I think she actually likes it that way.

'Let's get one thing straight,' I snap. 'I am not like you, not one little bit. I am not a mess – my life is under control. I'm slim, I'm disciplined, I'm successful – everything is right on track. What's the problem, Honey, are you jealous?'

Her face crumples. She snatches the cider shandy from my hands and drinks it down in one, throwing the paper cup into the bonfire as she walks away from me.

30

Did I really say those things? My heart is thumping as I try to gather my thoughts. Rude, cruel, careless, unkind . . . maybe I am more like Honey than I'd care to admit.

Tia and Millie and Skye pull me into the crush of people, quizzing me on today's audition, going over and over how much they will miss me. 'I don't want to think about that,' I tell them. 'Not yet.'

'You'll have to,' Tia shrugs. 'It's only a couple of weeks until school starts again. It won't be the same without you.'

'Shhh,' I say, pulling my friends up to dance on the sand. Someone has set up an iPod with portable speakers, and I dance for hours, long after Millie and Tia and Skye give up, exhausted. I kick off my shoes and dance with the warm sand in between my toes, whirling around in the dusk, trying to shut down the uncomfortable thoughts about the future that keep sliding into my mind.

When the speakers finally run out of charge, Shay plays guitar and Chris and Marty fetch African drums and a mouth organ from their caravan in the crew field, and it turns into a late-night jam session. There are toasted marshmallows and fruit punch and Honey's not-so-secret cider shandy, and people splinter away into little groups. Chris and Marty have paired up with a couple of the crew field girls, Skye and Finch are smooching down by the water's edge, Honey and JJ are holding hands by the fireside, and even Tia and Millie are doing some serious flirting with every unattached boy in the vicinity.

Coco's friends have gone home now and she is hanging on alone, arms wrapped round Humbug the lamb, stifling a yawn.

'Go up to the house, Coco,' I tell her. 'Take Humbug back to the stable.'

'Mmm,' Coco says. 'In a minute . . .'

I spot Alfie and Anthony sitting on a driftwood log a little way from the bonfire, and sit down beside them, worn out from dancing.

❀❀❀❀❀❀❀❀❀❀❀❀❀❀❀❀❀❀❀❀

'Hey,' Alfie says. 'Me and Anthony are setting the world to rights. Wanna join in?'

'Maybe. What are we talking about?'

'Your sister,' Anthony says heavily. 'I'm wasting my time with her, I think.'

'Honey?' I blink. 'I thought you were friends?'

'We are,' Anthony agrees. 'But that's all we'll ever be.'

'Never give up, mate,' Alfie says. 'There's always hope.'

We look across at Honey, who is leaning against JJ while talking to Marty and his girlfriend, twirling a strand of jaw-length blonde hair round her finger. Honey in full-on flirt mode is quite something. Marty seems to have forgotten he has a girlfriend, and Honey certainly seems to have forgotten about JJ.

'Maybe not,' Anthony says. 'It's late . . . I'm going to head off. Well done on the audition, Summer. G'night.'

Anthony mooches off into the darkness, and Alfie sighs. 'Not sure if that story's going to have a happy ending,' he says. 'But I am happy for you, Summer. I know how much you wanted that scholarship place.'

'It's not official yet,' I tell him.

✿✿✿✿✿✿✿✿✿✿✿✿✿✿✿✿✿✿✿✿✿

'As good as,' Alfie says. 'I'm pleased for you, but I will miss you, y'know.'

'Nobody to play practical jokes on?' I tease. 'Nobody to help you with your eyeliner?'

'I'm being serious,' he shrugs. 'No more trampoline marathons, no more heart-to-hearts, nobody to make daisy chains with . . .'

'You're rubbish at daisy chains anyhow,' I point out. 'Besides, I'll be back in the holidays . . . it's not like I'm emigrating!'

Not like my dad did, I think.

'I know,' Alfie grins. 'But . . . well, I have loved these last few weeks. I know it's been rough for you, with your mum away and what happened with Aaron and all the extra practice and . . . well, other stuff. But it's like I've had a chance to get to know you a bit. You've always been kind of distant, very ice princess . . .'

'Me?' I frown. 'Really?'

'Yup,' Alfie confirms. 'You're like the perfect girl, y'know? Cool, clever, endlessly talented, girl most likely to succeed . . . that stuff can be kind of daunting for us mere mortals.'

'I am so not perfect,' I say.

'You are to me . . .'

Alfie takes my hand in the darkness, and the tiniest crackle of electricity fizzes between us. It doesn't mean anything, of course. There could be no spark, no magic, with a boy like Alfie. Could there? And then he leans towards me and his lips are on mine, soft as velvet, warm as the night. Alfie tastes of sea salt and woodsmoke, and yes, there is a spark, a sizzle of fireworks that makes my heart race. How can that be? How can this kiss feel so different from my clumsy struggles with Aaron, me fending him off, him pushing closer? I was never good enough for Aaron, no matter how hard I tried. I was never enough, full stop.

Alfie's kiss is different, as different as the sun is from the moon. I don't want to push him away, I want to pull him closer – because with his arms around me I feel safe, calm, happy. Alfie's fingers stroke my hair, trace a path down my cheek, making me shiver.

What are you doing? the voice in my head sneers. *You must be crazy. He won't want you. Who would?*

I pull away, confused.

'Summer?' Alfie says. 'What's wrong?'

'N-nothing,' I stammer, blushing furiously in the darkness. 'I just . . . I'm not sure . . .'

I stand up, poised for flight. Honey was right – I am a mess, a girl in trouble, kidding herself she can control a life that is spinning wildly out of control. I spot JJ drinking cider alone in the firelight, Marty's girlfriend talking to her mates, Shay and Cherry, Skye and Finch, Sid and Carl and Tia and Millie. Honey and Coco are nowhere to be seen. Humbug the lamb trots up to me, butting my leg with his head, bleating softly.

'Where's Coco?'

'Think she went to bed,' Alfie says. 'Looks like she forgot Humbug. Summer, where are you going?'

I loop my skinny pink scarf round the lamb's neck and lead him to the cliff steps. 'I'll take him back,' I say over my shoulder. 'He'll be scared down here. Coco must have been really sleepy; she'd never normally leave him . . .'

But Alfie and I both know I am running away.

I climb the steps and walk across the moonlit garden, Humbug at my heels. An owl hoots and I can hear Fred the dog barking from inside the house, but the lights are off and I'm guessing Grandma Kate has gone to bed too. She trusts us. She doesn't know Honey is drinking cider shandy, flirting with two or three boys at once.

All is quiet as I push the door to Humbug's stable open and step from the bright moonlight into the darkness. Then Humbug pulls free and bolts out into the night, bleating. There's a scuffle, a cough and a yelp, two pinprick glows of red, the sound of someone swearing in the dark.

That's when I scream.

31

'Shut up, Summer! You'll wake the whole house!'

Honey has me by the shoulders, shaking me a little, her voice a hoarse whisper, her breath stinking of cider and smoke.

'What were you doing?' I squeak. 'You scared me half to death!'

'I wasn't doing anything,' she snaps. 'I just wanted a few minutes on my own! Is that a problem?'

'Of course not!' I argue. 'I just didn't expect . . .'

I trail away into silence, my head struggling to make sense of this. Honey hides out in a pitch-black stable in the middle of a beach party because she wants a few minutes on her own? It doesn't quite add up. Then I notice the shadowy figure in the doorway behind her, and it all makes sense again.

❀❀❀❀❀❀❀❀❀❀❀❀❀❀❀❀❀❀❀❀❀

'Hello, Marty,' I say. 'I think your girlfriend was looking for you. Come to think of it, Honey, JJ was looking for you too. And hey, here you both are . . .'

Marty holds his hands up in a gesture of surrender, a lit cigarette dangling from his fingers.

'Jen's not exactly my girlfriend,' he says. 'Not serious anyway. And Honey and I were . . . just talking really. No big deal. But . . . yeah. Whatever.'

He closes the stable door and walks past us in the moonlight, and I notice a smudge of Honey's red lipstick smeared across his cheek. Just talking? Not a chance.

'Marty, hang on,' my sister says. 'There's no need . . .'

'This wasn't a great idea,' he says over his shoulder. 'You're too young, and it's all too complicated. See you around . . .'

Honey's eyes brim with tears. 'Now look what you've done!' she growls. 'The first boy I've really liked in ages, and you have to ruin everything!'

'He's not exactly a boy,' I point out. 'He's a student – he must be at least nineteen. Besides . . . if Marty's so special, how come you've been wrapped round JJ all evening? That's wrong, Honey. You can't do stuff like this!'

✿✿✿✿✿✿✿✿✿✿✿✿✿✿✿✿✿✿✿✿✿✿

'Watch me.' She leans forward, pushing a finger towards the top of my chest, backing me up against the half-height stable door. 'I can do whatever I like. JJ doesn't own me! What's up, Summer, jealous because I'm having fun?'

'No, I . . .'

I catch the smell of smoke on her breath again, remember the pinpricks of red in the darkness. Two pinpricks of red.

'You've been smoking!' I whisper.

Honey laughs. 'So what? It was just a few drags. Not a crime, is it?'

Actually, smoking is pretty much a crime in our family. Mum's dad – Grandma Kate's first husband – died of lung cancer before we were even born, and Mum has always drummed it into us that smoking kills.

'Honey, no!' I wail. 'Smoking is really, really bad for you. Look what happened to Grandad. Are you trying to make yourself ill?'

My big sister laughs out loud. 'Listen to you!' she snaps. 'Little Miss Perfect, lecturing me about the dangers of smoking. Well, what about the dangers of starving yourself to death, Summer? The dangers of anorexia?'

233

Anorexia? The word slips under my skin like poison, seeping into my bones. That's not what has been happening to me, of course. It couldn't possibly be.

'Shut up!' I yell. 'I don't have . . . well, anything like that. You're crazy!'

'You can't even say it, can you?' Honey taunts me. 'But it's the truth, whether you like it or not. It's anorexia. You have an eating disorder, Summer. Fact. You're painfully thin. You look awful, you're tired all the time, and you're exercising way too much . . .'

'Stop it!' I protest, clamping my hands over my ears.

'I won't stop,' Honey says. 'You're wasting away, yet you're making all these mad calorie-laden dinners for the rest of us. Pizza, cupcakes, macaroni cheese . . . it's weird, Summer! Freaky! You don't eat a bite. I was watching you earlier, trying to choke down two measly mouthfuls of Grandma Kate's cake – anyone would think she'd given you rat poison to eat!'

I close my eyes. I want Honey to go away, shut up, leave me alone. She doesn't.

'I know what you're doing,' she says. 'I've watched you feeding your dinner to Fred, pushing stuff around your plate

234

so it looks like you're eating. I've been worried sick. Skye has noticed too, and Grandma Kate will catch on soon . . .'

'I've been stressed out, I know, but it's over now,' I argue. 'I'll be fine once Mum gets back!'

'She'll get the shock of her life when she sees you,' Honey says. 'So what – I had a drag on a cigarette. Big deal. You're the one who's making herself ill! You're throwing your life away!'

I take a deep breath, swaying slightly. I don't feel well. There is a knot of panic in my belly, the crackle of fear in my ears, the stink of smoke on every breath I take. Honey's eyes widen, and suddenly, the crackling sound, the stink of smoke, the sick feeling of panic begin to make sense.

'Oh my God . . . come away!' Honey screams. 'The hay's on fire!'

She pulls me away from the stable door, but not before I've seen the bright flicker of leaping flames, felt the heat on my face.

'Get help!' I yell. Honey and I both know that the stable's right next door to the chocolate workshop. 'Wake Grandma Kate, get the others, call the fire brigade . . .'

My sister is gone in a flash, running towards the house.

235

I could run to the cliff steps, yell for the others, but every moment wasted fetching help means the fire takes hold more. The stable is filled with hay, soft and dry and sweet. It will burn like paper. By the time the fire brigade arrive, the whole stable block will be burnt to the ground, including the workshop and all the stock and machinery Mum and Paddy have worked so hard for.

I remember the hosepipe Mum uses to water the vegetable garden, permanently hooked up to the outside tap. I run to the side of the house, open up the tap and drag the hosepipe towards the stable. I may not be able to put the fire out, but if I can damp it down, stop it from spreading, I could still save the workshop.

I open the stable door and a roar of flames, a wall of heat, leaps out at me. I have never been more scared in my life, but as long as I stay outside the stable, I should be safe. I point the hose and a jet of water arcs out, hissing as it sprays the orange flames. I can hear shouting from the house, the sound of feet on gravel.

The heat subsides a little and the flames shrink back. I step forward, into the doorway itself, my eyes streaming, stinging from the smoke. My fingers are ice-cold on the nozzle of the hosepipe, my lungs clogged. I feel light-headed for a moment, wobbly. I pull a deep breath in and struggle to hang on because this is the very last place I want to faint. That would be bad. Very, very bad.

'Summer!' Voices are calling me through the darkness. 'Summer, where are you?'

Then the ground tilts beneath my feet and I reach out for something to lean on, but the doorframe slides away from my grasp and I fall down on to blackened, sodden hay, the flames closing around me.

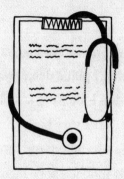

32

'Smoke inhalation,' the nurse says. 'That's probably why she passed out, although we can't be certain. There've been no known dizzy spells, no tendency to faint?'

'Not that I know of,' Grandma Kate answers. I know better, of course.

I am on a trolley bed in A & E, exhausted after being poked and prodded at and quizzed over and over. I reach up a hand to tug at the oxygen mask, but someone swats my hand away. 'It's there to help you,' the nurse says. 'How are you feeling? Not so woozy?'

I try to speak, but the oxygen mask gets in the way. 'Mmmm . . .'

'Perhaps we can do without that now,' the nurse decides.

❀❀❀❀❀❀❀❀❀❀❀❀❀❀❀❀❀❀❀

She turns to Grandma Kate. 'We've found a room on the wards for her so we can keep her under observation. You go home, get some sleep . . . I expect they'll discharge her in the morning.'

'Sleep tight,' Grandma Kate says. 'You gave us all such a fright, Summer. My mobile's been bleeping all night – the girls want you to know that the fire is out and the chocolate workshop is safe. You'll be home tomorrow, and Charlotte and Paddy too . . . no harm done.'

No thanks to me, I think. Honey may have dropped the cigarette, but only because I disturbed her; it flared up unseen because she and I were rowing.

A porter comes to wheel my trolley bed away from the bright lights of A & E, through antiseptic corridors to a curtained cubicle in a darkened ward. A different nurse comes to settle me in. 'Rest,' she tells me. 'Everything will look better in the morning.'

I wish I could believe that.

I close my eyes and the voice is in my head, whispering, taunting. *You've really messed up this time*, it says. *Idiot. Fool.*

At least now I know its name, know who is playing with

239

my head. The word beats through my veins like a pulse, inescapable.

Anorexia, anorexia, anorexia.

The hospital breakfast is disgusting: a slop of porridge with a crust of brown sugar on top, two slices of white toast with butter and jam. I cannot even look at it.

'Not hungry?' the nurse frowns. 'You have to eat, Summer. There's nothing of you!'

A doctor arrives and checks my breathing, my heart rate, my blood pressure, my weight. I am doing OK up until that last bit.

'You're underweight,' the doctor comments. 'Considerably so. Did you have breakfast?'

'I didn't like it,' I shrug.

'Do you often skip meals?'

'No, of course not!'

'And you're in here because you passed out cold while trying to put out a fire,' the doctor frowns, reading my notes. 'Do you often have dizzy spells?'

'No,' I say. 'Not often. Sometimes.'

'What had you eaten yesterday?' the doctor asks. I frown and try to think.

'An apple, early on,' I say. 'An egg, some lettuce. Two bites of cake . . .'

The doctor scribbles some notes and leaves, and a nurse appears to tell me that Grandma Kate has been delayed. She will be in this afternoon with Mum and Paddy. 'Can I go home then?' I plead.

The nurse won't meet my eye. 'We'll see,' she says. I turn my face away.

A little while later the curtain twitches and a boy appears, a boy with messy hair and kind brown eyes with cartoon lashes drawn on clumsily in eyeliner. He looks slightly deranged, but hey, that's nothing new.

'Alfie!' I say. 'What're you doing here? What's with the lashes?'

'Trying to make you laugh,' he says. 'And shhh. I'm undercover, OK? Visiting doesn't start until two, so I sneaked in.'

The last time I saw Alfie I'd just kissed him at the beach party. A slow blush seeps through my cheeks and I scrabble up into a sitting position, painfully aware of my hospital gown, my hair still fluffy from the pillow. I pick up my pink flower hairclip from the bedside table and slide it in.

'Gorgeous,' he says. 'And the flower's not bad either. One of my better ideas that was.'

My eyes widen, astonished, and Alfie's cheeks flood crimson. 'Oops,' he says. 'Did I just say that? I mean . . . very nice . . . whoever gave it to you. Aaron, or . . . well . . . whoever.'

'It was you, wasn't it?' I ask. 'It was you all along. And you never said. You let me think Aaron left the secret present. It was the sweetest, most romantic thing he ever did, and now it turns out it wasn't even him? Oh, Alfie . . .'

'Busted,' he shrugs. 'What can I say? And I brought you something else . . .'

He places a tiny bunch of daisies on the blue waffle bedspread, the stems wrapped in damp tissue. 'In case you want to make daisy chains,' he grins.

'Thanks,' I whisper. 'It was sweet of you to come. They'll be letting me out soon, but . . . thanks.'

'Right,' Alfie says. 'I walked up to Tanglewood earlier to see how you were, but it was just crazy, what with the police and the newspaper people and everything, and obviously your gran won't get in to see you till later now. So I thought I'd just jump on a bus and come say hi. In case you were worrying.'

'Police?' I echo. 'Newspaper people? I am worrying now, Alfie. What's happened?'

Alfie bites his lip. 'They didn't tell you?' he says. 'Right. No. They didn't tell you, obviously. Because you're ill in hospital with smoke inhalation and they don't want to stress you out . . .'

'Tell me what?' I say.

'I am a liability,' Alfie groans. 'I try to do the right thing, but then I just open my big mouth and put my foot in it, every single time . . .'

'Alfie, tell me!' I yell.

He goes a little pale. 'It's Honey,' he says. 'She went missing last night while the ambulance and the fire engine were there. Her passport's gone and money's been taken and your grandma is worried sick . . .'

My eyes widen. Mum and Paddy are due back any time. Will they return to find that a stable has burnt down and that one of their daughters is missing, the other in hospital? Nightmare.

'Why would she do that?' Alfie asks. 'Run away?'

243

'When I tried to put Humbug in the stable, Honey and Marty were in there,' I say. 'They'd been smoking – and, well, kissing, I think. Marty legged it and Honey chucked down her cigarette . . . We were arguing and didn't notice the fire till it was too late. She went to get help, and I was trying to keep the flames down, but I went all woozy and passed out . . .'

'I bet Honey blames herself,' Alfie says.

I sigh. 'She won't know whether the workshop was saved, or whether I'm OK, or anything. She must be worried sick . . .'

Alfie settles himself in the bedside armchair. 'She won't get far,' he says. 'She can't, can she? Where would she go?'

'I don't know.'

I think of the passport and my heart lurches. Surely nobody would sell an airline ticket to a fifteen-year-old? My sister is out there somewhere, a runaway . . . and all because of me. I pick up a daisy and pierce the stem with my thumb-nail, pushing another flower through, linking the daisies together and willing my big sister to stay safe, to come home. By the time I've linked all of the daisies, my eyes are blurred with tears.

'Epic fail on the cheer-up front,' Alfie says glumly. 'Useless, aren't I?'

'Not useless,' I tell him. 'Not useless at all.'

'You know I'm here for you, right?' he grins. 'Always. Just ask, just text, I'll be there. OK?'

The curtain flicks back and a nurse appears with a tray of food. She tries to chase Alfie away, but he says he is my cousin, then my brother, then my boyfriend, and finally the nurse takes pity on him and lets him stay. When she's gone, he watches me pick out a single lettuce leaf and leave the rest.

'Not hungry?'

'Just tired,' I sigh. 'I feel like I haven't slept for a month.'

'You have to eat,' he says, nicking a few forkfuls of pasta. 'You know that, don't you?'

'I can't,' I whisper.

'So tell someone,' Alfie says. 'Someone in here, someone who can help. Because I have waited a long time for you to notice me, Summer Tanberry, and I'm not about to lose you now.'

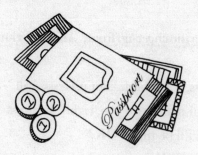

33

Alfie leaves, but before I can try to call anyone to find out what's happened with Honey, yet another doctor, young and pretty, with shiny dark hair and bright red lipstick, comes to talk to me. 'I'm Dr Khan,' she tells me. 'I specialize in working with young people with eating issues. Everyone is quite worried about you, you know.'

I bite my lip.

'Summer, are you on a diet?'

'Not exactly . . .'

'Watching what you eat?'

I shrug.

'Your parents have been out of the country for a while,'

she says, consulting her notes. 'They're coming in later to see you . . .'

'I thought I was going home?' My eyes brim with tears and the tears spill down my cheeks, on and on as if they will never stop.

'You will,' Dr Khan says. 'But a few things have come up, and I'd like to talk to your grandma first, and your parents. I believe you've lost a lot of weight lately. I don't think you're eating much at all, and that's almost certainly why you passed out last night. Your body is starving, Summer. I know you're frightened, and I know you're doing your best right now, but sometimes even the strongest and smartest of us need help. That's what I'm here for.'

Don't tell her, the voice in my head roars. *Don't!*

And then I hear an echo of Alfie's words, saying just the opposite. 'Tell someone. Someone who can help.'

'You don't understand,' I whisper. 'I can't help it. Any of it. I know it's scaring people, but I can't stop – I'm just trying to keep everything under control because it feels like nothing ever is! Is that so bad?'

Even as I say it, I begin to see that trying to survive on

❀❀❀❀❀❀❀❀❀❀❀❀❀❀❀❀❀❀❀❀❀❀

lettuce leaves and apples won't make me a better dancer or a better daughter. It won't take away the stress of competing for a place at dance school or a starring role, and it cannot turn the clock back to when I was seven years old or make my dad love me as much as I want him to.

'I do understand,' Dr Khan says softly. 'I understand because I've been there too, and I came through. You're clever, Summer, a perfectionist, a worker, just as I was. You like to have things under control, but trust me, this isn't the way to achieve your dreams. It can only destroy them, destroy everything you've worked so hard for.'

'I don't know what to do,' I say, the words salty with tears.

'I do,' Dr Khan says. 'I can help you. I promise.'

It's evening by the time Mum and Paddy arrive, their faces weary with jet lag and worry. Mum throws her arms round me and pulls me close.

'I'm sorry,' she whispers into my hair. 'I'm sorry I wasn't here when you needed me. Oh, Summer, what have you done to yourself?'

I cling on tight, my tears making a wet patch on the shoulder of her T-shirt, breathing in her familiar smell of coconut shampoo and love, letting her rock me, stroke my hair, hold me close.

'It's OK,' I whisper over and over, like a mantra. And somehow it is.

Paddy tells me that Honey has been found, that the police tracked her down to Heathrow, where she'd tried to buy a ticket for Australia with the emergency credit card taken from the kitchen drawer. 'She's safe,' he tells me, his face grim. 'That's something, I suppose.'

I look at the daisy chain made earlier, draped over the headboard of the hospital bed like a talisman. It is wilted now, but still, it's a comfort.

We all talk again with Dr Khan, who asks me to come to a weekly clinic where she can help me with my fear of food. 'Beating an eating disorder takes time,' she tells me. 'You need to be patient, determined. It will be hard work. But if you trust me, I can help you.'

'What about when term starts?' Paddy frowns. 'She'll be at boarding school then.'

'No,' Dr Khan says firmly. 'She won't. We have to tackle this first . . . Summer needs to get well.'

I wait for the pain of this to twist at my heart, but

❀❀❀❀❀❀❀❀❀❀❀❀❀❀❀❀❀❀❀❀

all I feel is relief. I cannot go to Rochelle Academy right now, I know that. I wouldn't last a week, let alone a month.

The next day I am allowed home. There is no welcome banner, no celebration cake, just wide eyes and wary looks and hugs that are so gentle they make me feel like I am made of glass and might shatter at any moment. Honey isn't there. Mum tells me she hasn't left her room since last night.

'Are you all right?' Cherry wants to know. 'Is there anything we can do?'

I shake my head, unable to find the words. I have taken our muddled, happy family and smashed it to pieces, painted blue shadows of worry under my mum's eyes, etched deep lines of fear into Grandma Kate's forehead. My twin is looking at me as though I am a stranger, as though she never knew me at all, and that hurts.

'I just want things to be normal,' I say. 'Carry on with your usual things. Cherry, go and see Shay. Coco, hang out with your friends. Skye, you're supposed to be working . . . don't stay home on my account, OK? Do whatever you'd usually be doing. I'm fine, honestly . . . but I'm really tired . . .'

Mum sighs. 'You're right, Summer . . . you should probably rest.'

I go up to my room, close the door softly. I pick up a ballet CD and slot it into the player, slip on my pointe shoes and tie the ribbons carefully. I stand with one hand on the window sill, chin tilted high, arms curved, feet in first position. Then the tears come, and I slam a hand down on the CD player to stop the music, tear off the shoes. I've been waiting for the pain to hit and now it's here, wave after wave of grief for a dream that will never be. I have ruined everything, sabotaged my future.

Mum will have to make awkward phone calls, talk to Miss Elise and Sylvie Rochelle. Another girl will get my scholarship place, my dream. Maybe Jodie? I hope so. At least then some good would have come from it all.

There's a knock at the door and Honey appears, her blonde hair ruffled, eyeliner smudged. 'We need to talk,' she says.

We sit at opposite ends of the bed, cross-legged, the patchwork cover stretched out between us.

❀❀❀❀❀❀❀❀❀❀❀❀❀❀❀❀❀❀❀

'I'm an idiot,' she begins. 'The worst big sister since time began. I'm so sorry, Summer. I was sick with worry when I found you in the stable, and then the ambulance came and it was all my fault . . .'

I shake my head. 'If I hadn't disturbed you, argued with you, none of this would have happened. And I fainted because I'd hardly eaten anything all day, not because of the smoke.'

Honey shrugs. 'I've been worried about you for weeks,' she says. 'I'm just not good at showing it. It's anorexia, Summer; you have to face up to it.'

I nod. 'There's a doctor at the hospital, a specialist. She's going to help me.'

'I hope so,' Honey says. 'Because I can't bear it, watching you disintegrate. I'm the disaster in this family, OK? I've just proved it once and for all, so don't even try to pretend you can come close. Running away sucks by the way. I met so many creeps I was almost glad when the police showed up.'

'Were you trying to get to Dad?'

She shrugs. 'I wanted to be as far away from here as possible, and I thought Dad might understand. As if. I spoke to him on Skype last night, and he was furious.'

'He's pretty hopeless, as dads go,' I say.

'I guess,' Honey says, and that's how I know she is really hurting because I have never heard her say a word against Dad before, not ever.

'I've crossed a line this time,' she goes on. 'Smoking, starting a fire, letting my little sister almost burn to death . . .'

'It wasn't like that,' I argue.

'It was a bit like that,' she says. 'And what do I do? Stay and face the music? No. I run away and end up in the middle of a major police hunt with headlines in the newspapers and everything. That's bad, even for me.'

I smile sadly.

'I'll be grounded until I'm about sixty, I suppose,' Honey grins. 'My life is over. Marty will never look at me now, or JJ. I might as well sign up for extra maths class and start dating Anthony.'

'Anthony's OK,' I say. 'You haven't treated him very well . . .'

'I don't treat anyone very well,' Honey admits. 'It's not my style. I'm a bitch, right? I don't care about anyone else . . .'

I squeeze Honey's hand. 'You do care . . . I know you do.'

She wipes a hand across her eyes, fierce, furious. 'Just be

careful, Summer,' she says. 'I'm the rebel and you're Little Miss Perfect, but it's just the same. You act a certain way and people expect you to go on doing it. It becomes the only way you know, and then you're trapped . . .'

I blink. All these weeks I've been looking for someone who might understand how I was feeling – I just never guessed it could be Honey. Both of us feel the same hurt; we just react to it differently. I bottle up the pain, get angry with myself, push myself harder and harder, looking for perfection; Honey rebels and lashes out, angry at the world, making the wrong choices time after time. So different, yet so alike. I wish I'd seen it before.

'We can change, can't we?' I say. 'I feel like I've been on a treadmill for years, pushing the whole time, trying to be perfect . . . but I can't quite get there. And right now, I'm tired of trying. I just want to be well again.'

My big sister holds me close. 'You will be,' she says.

34

Mum has made a huge feast of a dinner, a farewell meal for Grandma Kate and one designed to tempt me into eating. She makes all my one-time favourite foods: chicken pie and roast potatoes and gravy, with every kind of vegetable. Even Honey has helped, concocting a huge tower of meringue, whipped cream, strawberries and nuts. The table is heaped up like a Christmas feast, and my heart sinks because I know I can't eat this, can't even try.

'It's great to be back,' Mum says, breaking the silence. 'Peru was amazing, absolutely incredible, but . . . there's no place like home.'

'Trip of a lifetime,' Paddy says. 'And finding an organic cocoa supplier was the icing on the cake. It's a real family set-up. Our involvement will make all the difference to them, and we get the boost of having an organic Fairtrade product too . . .'

'Wonderful,' Grandma Kate says. And then the conversation crashes.

'Aren't you eating, Summer?' Mum cajoles. 'Just a little? I want to feed you up now that I'm home . . .'

I hang my head, panic rising inside me. There is just too much of everything, and besides, I don't want to be 'fed up'. I spear a green bean and try to eat it, fail. I put my fork down.

I thought I would feel better, facing up to the problem, agreeing to get help. Isn't that meant to be the hardest part? I thought some kind of magic switch would flick on and I would begin to get better, that the fears would lift and I could eat again, but that hasn't happened.

'You're scaring her,' Skye says, picking up on my mood. 'This isn't going to work.'

I scrape my chair back roughly and get up, pushing out of the kitchen. I run up the stairs, find my mobile and punch out a message. A reply pings back almost at once, and I smile.

I push a small bundle into my pink shoulder bag and go

downstairs again, sneaking out of the front door and across the grass, beneath the trees and down to the cliff path. I pick my way down the steps, kick off my shoes, walk down to the sea. The tide has turned, leaving a margin of damp sand, ridged and ribbed, edged with surf. I wade into the water, shivering as a swirl of seaweed tangles around my ankles, feeling the push and pull of the ocean.

I reach into my pink shoulder bag and my fingers close round the new satin pointe shoes I had for my audition. My eyes blur with tears. I lift out the shoes, flinging them in a graceful arc across the waves so that the ribbons fly out behind them like streamers. They land randomly in the surf, buffeted backwards and forwards by the tide, getting further and further from the shore.

I am not going to ballet school, not now, maybe not ever. I'm not sure I even care any more. Mum mentioned something about studying dance after A levels, taking a performing arts course or training to be a dance teacher, but right now, I can't think that far ahead.

The girl most likely to succeed . . . that's a laugh. The dreams are over, shot down in flames, and I have nobody to blame but myself.

✿✿✿✿✿✿✿✿✿✿✿✿✿✿✿✿✿✿✿

I feel like my heart is breaking. I turn away from the ocean, and in the distance I see Alfie walking along the sand towards me.

'You came,' I say, once he is close enough to hear me.

'Of course I came,' he says simply. 'You asked me to.'

'I messed up,' I tell him. 'Already. I want to get well again, I really do, but Mum made a special meal for me and everyone was looking at me and I couldn't eat any of it . . .'

'Hey,' Alfie says. 'Early days. You have to take it slowly. Give it a chance – this doctor person hasn't even started helping you yet. You can do it, Summer. Believe it.'

He pushes a rucksack into my arms. 'Anyhow, I brought supplies . . .'

We spread a blanket on the sand, unpack strawberries, apples, hard-boiled eggs, even a strange-looking cake that dips a little in the middle. 'It's carrot cake,' he explains. 'My own recipe. Wholemeal flour, no sugar, extra-low-fat cream cheese frosting . . .'

We sit side by side on the beach, looking out to sea. I eat a hard-boiled egg, an apple, and it doesn't feel scary and the voice in my head stays silent. I bite into a strawberry, letting the sweet juice stain my lips. Alfie slips an arm round my shoulder and I lean into him, relaxing. I wonder if he will kiss me again, and if the kiss will taste of strawberries.

If I look hard enough, I can still see the pointe shoes, bobbing slightly on the current, far out to sea.

'I won't be going to ballet school now,' I tell Alfie. 'That dream bit the dust.'

'OK,' he says. 'Plan B then.'

'There is no Plan B,' I sigh.

'Better think of one then. And if Plan B falls through, move on to Plan C. There are twenty-six letters in the alphabet, right? You're not a quitter, Summer.'

'I guess.'

Alfie slices a piece of carrot cake, the tiniest piece ever, and offers it to me. I break off a corner and take a bite. It's lighter than it looks, moist and sweet and fresh-tasting.

'It's good,' I say, surprised.

'Yup,' he grins. 'I've given up on the celebrity chef idea. I'm aiming more for the healthy wholefood market now. Plan D I think that is, for me.'

Broken dreams . . . maybe they're just stepping stones to new possibilities? I like that idea.

Alfie leans across and kisses me then, swiftly, gently. He

tastes of carrot cake and strawberries and hope, and that makes me smile. I am not sure you could ever have enough of a kiss like that.

'Hey. I made something else for you,' he says, taking something from the side pocket of his rucksack. 'It took forever because my fingers are all clumsy and slow, but . . .'

He holds out a daisy-chain circlet and puts it in my hair, tucked behind the pink silk flower, a princess-crown, fragile, perfect.

Resources

If you are worried about an eating disorder, please talk to a parent, teacher or to your family doctor and get some adult help and support. As Summer comes to realize, controlling your food cannot solve your problems – it will only add to them.

If you are worried about a friend, talk to a trusted teacher and share your concerns, in confidence if need be. Letting an adult know is important, as an eating disorder is easier to treat when spotted early on.

Remember that diets of any kind are bad news for teens or pre-teens; your body is still developing and restricting calories can cause real damage. If you genuinely feel you need help with your weight, please see your family doctor.

Websites:

www.b-eat.co.uk – help and support for anyone worried about an eating disorder

www.eatingdisorderssupport.co.uk – confidential support for anyone with an eating disorder

www.eating-disorders.org.uk – beating anorexia, bulimia, binge-eat disorder, etc.

www.evamusby.co.uk – for parents worried about a child with anorexia

Email support:

support@eatingdisorderssupport.co.uk

UK helplines:

Beat Youthline: 0845 634 7650

Eating Disorders Support: 01494 793223

Books:

Letters To Cathy by Cathy Cassidy – help and advice on self-esteem, confidence and learning to accept and like yourself, plus support with many other growing-up issues.

A gorgeous new series by

Cathy Cassidy

The Chocolate Box GIRLS

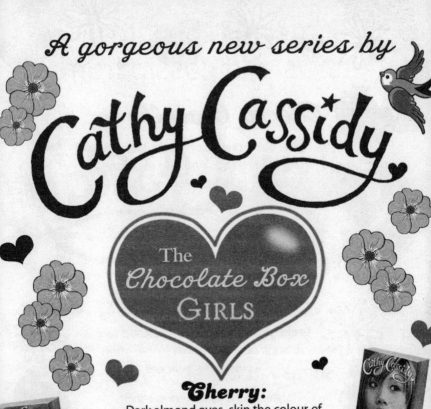

Cherry:
Dark almond eyes, skin the colour of
milky coffee, wild imagination, feisty, fun . . .

Skye:
Wavy blonde hair, blue eyes, smiley, individual, kind . . .

Summer:
Slim, graceful, pretty, loves to dance, determined, a girl with big dreams . . .

Coco:
Blue eyes, fair hair, freckles, a tomboy who loves
animals and wants to change the world . . .

Honey:
Willowy, blonde, beautiful, arty and out of control, a rebel . . .

*Each sister has a different story to tell,
which will be your favourite?*

Cherry Costello is ...

shy, quiet, always on the outside . . .
sometimes finds it hard to separate
truth from fiction

14 years old

Born: Glasgow

Mum: Kiko

Dad: Paddy

Looks: small; slim; coffee-coloured skin;
straight, dark hair with a fringe, often
worn in little bunches

Style: bright skinny jeans, T-shirts,
anything with a Japanese theme

Loves: dreaming, stories, cherry blossom,
Irn-Bru, gypsy caravans

Prize possessions: kimono, parasol,
Japanese fan, photo of her mum
from long ago

Dreams: of being part of a family

www.cathycassidy.com

Skye Tanberry is ...

friendly, eccentric, individual, imaginative

13 years old - Summer's identical twin

Born: Kitnor

Mum: Charlotte

Dad: Greg

Looks: shoulder-length blonde hair,
blue eyes, big grin

Style: floppy hats and vintage dresses,
scarves and shoes

Loves: history, horoscopes,
dreaming, drawing

Prize possessions: her collection
of vintage dresses and the fossil
she once found on the beach

Dreams: of travelling back in
time to see what the past
was really like . . .

www.cathycassidy.com

Summer Tanberry is ...

quiet, confident, pretty, popular,
and very serious about dance

13 years old - Skye's identical twin

Born: Kitnor

Mum: Charlotte

Dad: Greg

Looks: long blonde hair, always tied
back in braids or a neat ballerina bun;
blue eyes; moves gracefully

Style: anything pink . . . neat, pretty,
fashionable clothes and dance-wear

Loves: dancing, especially ballet

Prize possessions: pointe shoes and tutu

Dreams: of going to the Royal Ballet
School, becoming a professional
dancer and one day running her
own ballet school

Coco Tanberry is ...

cheeky, energetic, friendly,
adventurous, crazy about animals

12 years old

Born: Kitnor

Mum: Charlotte

Dad: Greg

Looks: chin-length wavy blonde hair,
always tangled; blue eyes; freckles;
big grin

Style: tomboy: jeans, T-shirt, always
messy and dishevelled

Loves: animals, climbing trees,
swimming in the sea

Prize possessions: Fred the dog
and the ducks

Dreams: of having a llama,
a donkey and a parrot

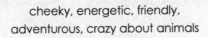
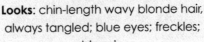

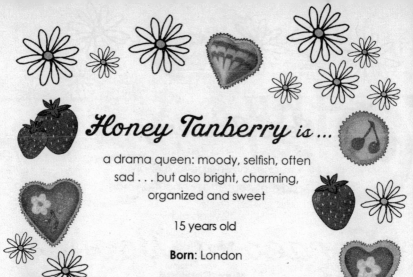

Honey Tanberry is ...

a drama queen: moody, selfish, often sad . . . but also bright, charming, organized and sweet

15 years old

Born: London

Mum: Charlotte

Dad: Greg

Looks: long, ringletty blonde hair that reaches to her waist; blue eyes; creamy skin; tall; slim

Style: cool: little print dresses, strappy sandals, shades, shorts and T-shirts

Loves: drawing, painting, fashion, music . . . and Shay Fletcher

Prize possessions: hair, diary, sketchbook, turret bedroom

Dreams: of being a model, actress or fashion designer

Follow your *Dreams* with all

Cathy Cassidy's

Gorgeous Books!

Which Chocolate Box Girl Are You?

Your perfect day would be spent . . .

a) visiting a busy vintage market
b) with your favourite canine companion on a long walk in the countryside
c) curled up on the sofa watching black-and-white movies with your boyfriend
d) window-shopping with your BFF
e) sipping frappuccinos in a hip city cafe

Your ideal boy is . . .

a) arty and sensitive
b) boy? No thanks!
c) a good listener . . . and a little bit quirky
d) polite and clever
e) good looking and popular – what other kind of boy is there?

Who's the first person you would tell about your new crush?

a) your sister – she knows everything about you
b) your pet cat . . . animals are great listeners
c) your BFF
d) your mum – she always has the best advice
e) no one. It's best not to trust anyone with a secret

Your favourite subject is . . .

a) history
b) science
c) creative writing
d) French
e) drama

Your school books are . . .

a) covered in paisley-print fabric
b) a bit muddy
c) filled with doodles
d) neat, tidy and full of good grades
e) rarely handed in on time

When you grow up you want to be . . .

a) an interior designer
b) a vet
c) a writer
d) a prima ballerina
e) famous

People always compliment your . . .

a) individuality. If anyone can pull it off you can!
b) caring nature – every creature deserves a bit of love
c) wild imagination . . . although it can get you into trouble sometimes
d) determination. Practice makes perfect
e) strong personality. You never let anyone stand in your way

Mostly As . . . *Skye*
Cool and eclectic, friends love your relaxed boho style and passion
for all things quirky.

Mostly Bs . . . *Coco*
A real mother earth, but with your feet firmly on the ground, you're
happiest in the great outdoors – accompanied by a whole menagerie
of animal companions.

Mostly Cs . . . *Cherry*
'Daydreamer' is your middle name . . . Forever thinking up crazy stories and
buzzing with new ideas, you always have an exciting tale to tell – you're
allowed a bit of artistic licence, right?

Mostly Ds . . . *Summer*
Passionate and fun, you're determined to make your dreams come
true . . . and your family and friends are behind you every step of the way.

Mostly Es . . . *Honey*
Popular, intimidating, lonely . . . everyone has a different idea about the
'real you'. Try opening up a bit more and you'll realize that friends are there
to help you along the way.

How can you make your WISHES and DREAMS ❤ come TRUE? ❤

WISHES and DREAMS are just other words for positive thinking, and that's something that can be very powerful. Get together with friends and create some beautiful dream flags to start the magic . . .

You will need:

✦ A3 white or coloured paper

✦ Coloured crayons, felt pens, oil pastels, water-based paints, brushes, scissors, glue, glitter, sequins, yarn, foil streamers, tinsel, stickers, stars, tissue paper, ribbon, gold/silver pens, assorted collage materials

✦ A long length of string/coloured cord/ribbon

✦ IMAGINATION!!!

How to make your DREAM FLAG:

✦ Take your piece of A3 paper and cut it in half lengthways. Then fold each piece in half so you have two long thin strips of paper. This will give you 2 flags.

✦ Use paints, pens, crayons, pastels or a combination to pattern/colour the paper. Or collage your flag with ribbon, foil, stars and paper.

✦ Write your dream on to the flag shape. If you'd rather keep the dream secret, just decorate the flag with your own patterns and symbols, but think about your dream while you are doing this.

✦ Use both sides of the flag, or get your friend to use the other side so you can share the dream flag!

✦ Fold your flag over the string/cord and staple or glue your flag into place . . . then hang the dream flags along a wall or classroom!

Coco's Lemonade

You need:

1 cup sugar
4–6 fresh lemons

Method:

Place one cup of sugar in a heatproof mixing jug and add one cup of boiling water, stirring gently until the sugar dissolves.

Use a lemon squeezer to squeeze the juice of 4–6 fresh lemons, enough to make a cupful.

Mix sugar-water and lemon juice together in a tall jug/pitcher and add 3–4 cups of water to taste.

Refrigerate for 30 mins and serve with lots of ice and slices of lemon.

For pink lemonade, slice up a bowlful of fresh strawberries and stir into the finished lemonade instead of lemon slices.

Find more yummy recipes at
www.cathycassidy.com

Yummy Ice-cream Sundaes

Banana Split

You need:
1 banana
vanilla ice cream
chopped nuts
chocolate sauce

Method:
Slice the banana in half lengthways, place in a dish and arrange three scoops of vanilla ice cream between the halves.

Decorate with a sprinkle of chopped nuts and a squoosh of chocolate sauce!

Chocolate Heaven

You need:
3 chocolate chip cookies, crumbled
4 squares chocolate, grated
vanilla ice cream
chocolate ice cream
chocolate sauce
aerosol cream

Method:
In a tall glass, layer a scoop of vanilla ice cream, a sprinkle of crumbled cookie, a scoop of chocolate ice cream and a layer of grated chocolate, and another scoop of vanilla ice cream and a layer of crumbled cookie. Top with a layer of squishy aerosol cream and decorate with grated chocolate and sauce . . . bliss!

Strawberry Sundae

You need:
fresh strawberries
plain frozen yoghurt
strawberry yoghurt
strawberry sauce

Method:
Cut most of the fresh strawberries into quarters then layer in a tall glass with the plain frozen yoghurt, strawberry yoghurt and an occasional squirt of strawberry sauce.

Repeat the layers until you reach the top of the glass. Finish off with the leftover strawberries and an extra squoosh of strawberry sauce!

www.cathycassidy.com

Summer Fruit Skewers

For a refreshing healthy snack on those hot summer days, try making your own garden of fruit skewers.

You will need:

Your fave fruits (the best ones include kiwis, strawberries, grapes, oranges, and watermelon and pineapple slices)

10 or more wooden skewers

Heart, flower or butterfly cookie cutters

A shoe box (this will be your garden display)

What to do:

Using a chopping board carefully cut your chosen fruit into round shapes.

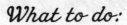

One at a time, lay your slices of fruit on the board and cut into flower, butterfly and heart shapes using the cookie cutters.

Carefully insert the skewers into the fruit to create a beautiful flower display.

Making a Flower:

Cut a slice of pineapple into a flower shape and add to the skewer so it's horizontal. Then add a small strawberry to the very top to make the centre of the flower. Add a couple of grapes to the 'stem' of the flower to look like leaves. Try other methods and designs too!

Assemble your Flower Garden:

Decorate your shoe box to make it look like a garden, using green paint, tissue paper, flower stickers, etc.

Cut small holes into the top of the shoe box.

Insert your flower skewers into the holes to create a flower border!

Top Tip!
For an extra-refreshing taste, serve with a yoghurt or cream-cheese dip!

*Here's where
it all started
in Cathy's
notebook . . .*

What Cathy Cassidy's fans think ...

'I LOVE your books . . . I can't put them down' *Leyla*

'I can't wait until Coco Caramel!
You're my favourite author EVER!!' *Ellen*

'I can't wait till your other books come out,
The Chocolate Box Girls are the best!' *Ruby*

'Me and my best friend have read all of your books!' *Isabelle*

'I'm obsessed with reading your books – they are
just THE BEST! You rock Cathy!' *Momin*

More praise for Cathy!

'I was addicted to *Marshmallow Skye* . . . beautiful,
perfect and super moreish' thebookaddictedgirl.blogspot.com

'Writing as engaging as this is not easy to pull off' *Mail on Sunday*

'A great choice for older Jacqueline Wilson fans' *Irish Independent*

'Wittily written . . . from the heart' *Radio Times*

Write your own review at www.cathycassidy.com

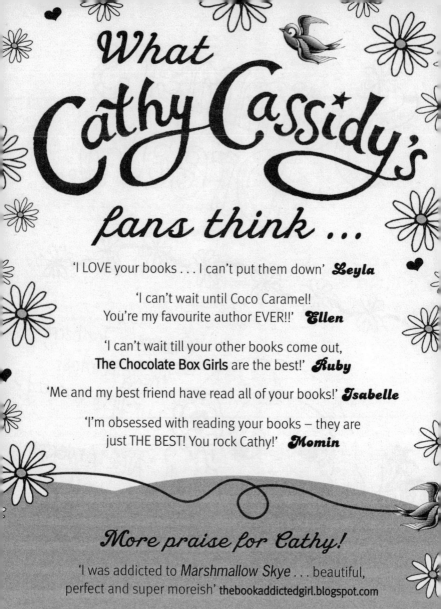